# Just One More Dare

## The Sterling Family
## Book 2

*NEW YORK TIMES BESTSELLING AUTHOR*
# Carly Phillips

Dear Reader (especially those already familiar with the Dare family):

As many of you know, Samantha was in Dare to Love and Dare to Desire and somehow along the way she got dropped as a character ... I eventually went back and edited out Samantha for continuity's sake. Chalk it up to human error. But people who had the original books have written and asked me for her story. For a long time, I had no plans to write her until one day, Dex Sterling needed a heroine and Samantha seemed like the perfect choice. So JUST ONE MORE DARE brings you Samantha Dare's story at last.

That said, many years have passed and despite re-reading, you may find inconsistencies. For example, in JUST ONE MORE DARE, Samantha is part of the "Original Dares", not the second family. Apologies but it fit better going forward that she be deeply connected to Ian.

In addition, I like to say that for me and many other writers, storyline and age occurs like they do in Soap Operas – it's called SORAS – Soap Opera Rapid Aging Syndrome. You can look forward to that with the kids of our hero and heroines of early books along with adding in Samantha.

I hope you'll understand and enjoy the story for what it is. I love Samantha and Dex.

Best,
Carly

# Chapter One

SAMANTHA DARE'S STOMACH churned with anxiety. She recognized the feeling, one she'd become familiar with as her wedding day approached. She'd tried to shake it off and did the same now, reminding herself that marrying her business partner was the smart thing to do. Just because the passion had fizzled didn't mean they wouldn't have a solid relationship based on shared interests.

She smoothed the lace bodice of the ballroom wedding gown she wore and chewed on her bottom lip.

"Samantha, are you okay?" her older sister, Olivia, asked. "Stop that or you're going to need to touch up your lipstick."

"I'm fine." She patted her bare lips. Dammit. She would need to have it put on again.

"Spill," Olivia persisted. "I know all your tells."

Their conversation caught the attention of Samantha's other bridesmaids: her sister, Avery, her half-sister, Sienna, her cousins, Lucy and Brianne, and Samantha's best friend and office manager, Brandy. They sat on the sofa and club chairs, picking from the charcuterie board filled with a variety of cheese, smoked meat, and tiny fruit. Half-empty champagne glasses were spread around the table. All the women looked beautiful in differing metallic colors with a variety of silhouettes.

Once Samantha became the center of attention, they all questioned her at the same time.

"Stop, I'm fine!" Samantha raised her voice and immediately regretted it. "Sorry. I'm just having nervous, walking-down-the-aisle jitters." She sighed. "I need some fresh air and a few moments alone to clear my head."

The bridal suite was located on the fourth floor of the Meridian NYC Hotel, on the same floor as the ballroom where the ceremony would occur. The hotel was once owned by her father, a man she neither respected nor wanted to think about on her special day. The Meridian Hotel Group was now in the hands of her cousins, something that worked for the entire family, so no hard feelings for anyone… except her father, Robert Dare.

The door to the terrace was already open and she stepped outside, then walked to the balcony. Bracing her hands on the top of the heavy stone railing, she drew a deep breath of beautiful spring air and wondered why she couldn't calm down.

Her gut told her it wasn't every day wedding jitters

but voices from another terrace distracted her and she focused on those instead of the unwelcome thoughts running through her mind. All would be well once she said *I do.*

"I know what you promised me," a distraught-sounding female said, the voice coming from the terrace around the corner from the one where Samantha stood.

Curious, Samantha couldn't help but step closer. Was she eavesdropping? Yes, but better to focus on someone else's issues than her own.

"But seeing you in this tuxedo, ready to get married... I don't like it," the woman continued, but now Samantha thought she recognized the voice. Marley, her soon-to-be husband's personal assistant, was speaking.

"We had an understanding." And *that* coaxing reply came from Samantha's fiancé, Jeremy Rollins.

"How long will it take before you're able to get rid of her?" Marley asked.

Shocked, Samantha's belly fluttered with nerves. Certain she'd misheard, she waited to hear her fiancé's reply—and what the hell was he doing alone with Marley right before their wedding, anyway?

"Calm down," Jeremy said in the patronizing voice Samantha hated. No woman liked being talked down to. "We've waited this long, surely you can hold out another year or two. The breakup has to look real if I'm going to get my hands on any of her money. Her brothers will make sure of *that*," he muttered. "It's you I love, Marley."

Silence descended, followed by an obvious-sounding moan.

Samantha sucked in a horrified breath. That no-good, low-life, cheating son of a bitch. He was having an affair with his personal assistant. The same woman he insisted he needed with him when he traveled to meet clients. He'd claimed his ADHD kicked in during long meetings and Marley took the most detailed notes. And Samantha had believed him.

She squeezed her eyes shut and pressed her hand to her rolling stomach. She was an idiot. He'd duped her into using her trust fund money to start their joint PR firm and she'd agreed, believing he was the brains when it came to creating potential campaigns. After they'd launched, his ideas had impressed many big-name clients to join them. Jeremy was smart. Apparently smart enough to put one over on her.

She lifted her skirt and stormed back into the suite, his false words ringing in her ears. *I love you, Samantha. We're going to be such a great team, Samantha. We have so much in common. We're a dynamic duo, Samantha.*

"Bullshit," she muttered, fury coursing through her veins.

"Samantha? What's wrong?" Her mother, Emma St. Claire, strode over.

Wearing a beautiful silver beaded gown, looking elegant as ever, her mother was Samantha's rock. There was no one she admired more for her strength and dignity, especially after everything her ex-husband had put her through. She was married a second time and extremely happy.

"Samantha?" Emma repeated, lines creasing her forehead, her concern obvious.

Samantha shook her head, already feeling the heaviness in her throat and the angry tears welling up in her eyes. "I don't... I can't... This wedding isn't happening."

"What? Why not?"

Samantha wasn't sure whose voice she heard the loudest as her family shouted questions her way.

Brandy strode over and grasped her hand. "Give me a few minutes," she said to everyone else. "Let me talk to her."

"Go ahead," Olivia said softly.

But her mother shook her head, clearly wanting to hear the problem now. Despite her hurt and anger, Samantha managed a smile. She wouldn't shut her mom out. The same with her sisters.

She squared her shoulders. "I just overheard my bastard fiancé reassuring his mistress that they'll be together one day, she just needs to be patient. To give him time to stay married long enough to get my money."

She ground her teeth as her family exploded in righteous anger on her behalf. "I need to go," Samantha said.

"Where?" her mom asked.

"To have a word with my *fiancé* and then I need to get out of here. I can't…" She sniffed, a small piece of her heart breaking at what a fool she'd been. "I can't face everyone. Especially Ian." Her brother, well, brothers plural, if she was being honest, had never liked Jeremy. Apparently, they had better taste and instincts than she had.

If Ian only knew how badly she'd nearly screwed up… As the oldest, he'd been like a parent to all the Dare kids, first when their father was traveling for business, and later, after he'd dropped the bomb that shattered their lives. That he had a second family nobody knew about. Ian would be so disappointed in her.

"Do you want me to go with you?" Brandy asked.

Samantha shook her head. "Thanks for the offer but I'm too afraid you'll punch him in the face before I get a chance to tell him to go fuck himself." If nothing else, Samantha was surrounded by a solid support system. So why hadn't she listened to their subtle but honest comments about the man she'd planned to marry?

She'd have plenty of time to ponder and figure out the whys later. "I'm sorry, everyone. I just…"

Her mother placed her hands on Samantha's shoulders. "You will be fine. Go do what you need to do and I'll handle the rest. But call or text and let us know where you decide to go. I want to know you're okay."

Samantha nodded. "I will. Thanks, Mom." She hugged her mother, taking comfort in the familiar scent of her perfume, then did the same with her sisters and cousins.

Brandy walked her to the suite door. "Are you sure you don't want support? I won't deck him until after you tell the bastard off."

Laughing, Samantha shook her head. "No thanks, but I love you for offering." She headed out the door, walked down the hall and around the corner leading to the groom's suite.

Stopping outside the door, she raised her hand to knock, pausing when she realized it was quiet inside. She supposed it made sense. If Jeremy wanted to be able to talk to his mistress, he'd probably sent his groomsmen away so they'd have some time alone.

At the reminder, she rapped on the door with her knuckles and when the bastard didn't open it immediately, she knocked hard again.

"David, I told you I needed time alone!" He opened the door partway, obviously expecting to see his best man. "Samantha! What are you doing here? It's bad luck for us to see each other before the ceremony."

"Since when are you superstitious?" She slammed her hand on the door, surprising him by pushing it open. She lifted her skirt once more, walked inside, and looked around the empty room. "Where is she?"

"Samantha, darling, what are you doing here?" He reached out his hand to touch her.

She snapped, slapping him across the face. "You bastard."

He reared back, holding his cheek in his hand. "What was that for?"

"For screwing your assistant behind my back," she said, with her heart pounding hard inside her chest.

He opened his mouth and she shook her head. "Don't. Our balconies are right next door to each other and I heard every word."

His cheeks highlighted with color. "Whatever you heard, you misunderstood. She was wishing us good luck. I love you, darling."

"Again, don't. Don't darling me. Don't patronize me. Don't try to twist what I heard or lie about the fact that you were marrying me for my money, you asshole." She worked the engagement ring off her finger and held it in front of his face. "The wedding is off."

"But—"

He didn't deserve another second of her time. She tossed the ring at him, turned, and walked to the door, ignoring his pleas to let him explain.

She returned to the bridal suite to find her bridesmaids in the midst of changing into their regular clothes when she walked in.

"Samantha!" her cousin Lucy said. "What happened?"

"I slapped him, threw the ring, and left. Now I'm here for my luggage." The plan had been for a hotel bellman to bring her bags up to the honeymoon suite for the wedding night. She was grateful that at least she'd have clothes wherever she decided to go to think about how she'd gotten to this place in her life.

"Good for you," her mother said. "Jeremy had better hope none of your brothers run into him because—"

"They know already?" she asked, feeling the heat rise to her cheeks.

Her mother grasped her hand. "Honey, they need to know in order to explain to the guests. But don't worry, they won't reveal why there won't be a wedding."

"Unless you want them to," Olivia said. "In which case, Dylan and your brothers would be more than happy to take him on in front of everyone." Her husband was as much part of the family as their blood relatives.

She pressed her fingers to the throbbing in her temples. "I can't handle this. I'm just going to change clothes and get out of here."

"You don't have time," Avery said. "Ian is on his way up. He's hoping to talk to you before you leave."

Dammit. The last person she wanted to face right now was the sibling she thought would be the most disappointed in her. "I need to leave."

"Come on." Brandy, the best friend ever, strode out of the bedroom, wheeling Samantha's luggage behind her. "I'll walk you downstairs and play body-guard. If anyone tries to question you I'll—"

"Beat them up?" Samantha laughed despite the pain in her heart; she refused to believe there was also relief.

In order to avoid her brother, they took the stairs and paused by the revolving doors in the hotel lobby. So far, they hadn't run into anyone they knew Samantha intended to keep it that way with a brief goodbye.

She turned to Brandy. "Thanks for being you." She hugged her friend, well aware the tears she'd been holding back were welling again.

"You'd better keep in touch when you figure out a plan. Where are you going?" Brandy asked.

Samantha pulled back and tried to blot her eyes with her fingertips. "I can't go home since I live with the asshole. Maybe a hotel? I'll let you know where I land."

Before her friend could ask more questions, Samantha grabbed the handle of her luggage and headed out the doors. Tears she hadn't let fall did just that, blurring her vision as she rushed forward, hoping to find a taxi instead of digging for her phone so she could order a rideshare and have to wait.

"Miss?" the valet called out, and she glanced over to see a car driving directly toward her.

She spun out of the way, twisting her foot in her high heels. The pain shot through her ankle as it gave way, causing her to fall to the ground in a heap, surrounded by her white, fluffy wedding dress.

# Chapter Two

DEX STERLING DROVE through the streets of Manhattan, drumming his fingers on the steering wheel of his new Benz G-Wagon. U2's haunting lyrics blasted, taking him back to his go-to playlist and how he'd get pumped up to receive the first snap of the game every Sunday for the Miami Thunder.

Did he miss football since retiring this past season? Yes. How could he not miss a sport that had been part of his life for decades? Along with the locker room comradery and everything that went along with success. But unlike many other trophy-winning players who dragged out retirement, Dex was content going out uninjured and with a winning record.

He'd invested well and saved both his salary and bonuses, along with the money his birth parents had left in trust when they died in a car accident when Dex was seven years old. He'd then gone to live with new guardians, his next-door neighbors, Alex and Gloria Sterling, the parents of his best friend, Remy.

When Dex turned ten, they'd offered to adopt him, and as he'd always felt like one of the family and wanted the relationships to be real, he'd agreed. He'd been too young then to know about trust funds but today, as a Sterling, he now had even more money to his name. Which meant Dex had his choice of next steps.

He'd recently accepted the position of lead analyst at FSN (Football Sports Network), the top football sports channel, and was headed to meet Wes Johnson, a former teammate, also retired, who wanted to talk about investing in a new clothing brand.

Dex turned into the circular drive of the Meridian NYC where Wes was staying. Sunbeams streamed between two buildings, immediately hitting his eyes and all but blinding him for precious seconds. As soon as he could see again, a woman in a cloud of white material surrounding her stepped in front of his vehicle and he slammed on the brakes.

She spun too fast and fell to the ground, disappearing from sight.

"Shit!" But he hadn't hit her. He hoped. After jamming the vehicle in park, he flung open the door and climbed out, rushing to where she'd gone down.

The doorman was already fussing over her, insisting he call an ambulance.

"I wasn't hit," she argued. "Just startled."

Dex stepped closer. "Are you really okay?" he asked, as familiar indigo blue eyes looked up at him and recognition dawned. "Samantha?"

He was surprised to realize he'd almost hit Ian Dare's youngest sister. Ian, the Thunder team owner and Dex's former boss. And the man who'd blocked any shot Dex could have had with Samantha years before. Just recently, he'd heard from Ian, who was now a good friend, that his sister was getting married, but Dex hadn't known where, when, or to whom. Truth be told, he'd tried to block the entire thing from his mind.

"Dex! Small world," she said, as he helped her to her feet, wincing as she stood. "I twisted my ankle," she muttered, leaning down, lifting her skirt and pulling off her heels.

She was as beautiful as he remembered, her blonde hair falling to her shoulders, clipped behind her head with a white bow. Her skin was a gleaming porcelain, with a hint of blush, and a smoky look to her eyes.

She was stunning. And marrying another man.

"Shouldn't you be inside… I don't know, getting married or something?" His voice sounded unnecessarily harsh.

She flinched, his words causing her eyes to open wide. As if remembering where she was and why. "No, that's the last thing I want to do." She glanced back over her shoulder then met his gaze. "Get me out of here, Dex? Please?" She blinked and a tear dropped down her face.

"Samantha!" A man in a tuxedo stepped out of the revolving hotel entrance.

She grabbed Dex's hand and a jolt of something powerful ran up his arm. "Please," she said, desperation in her tone. "Let's just *go*."

He groaned, knowing what he was going to do even before he'd consciously made the decision, aware it could possibly bring the wrath of Ian Dare down on his head.

Dex opened his car door. "Get in."

"Samantha, you misunderstood everything. Let me explain," the other man, obviously her groom, called out just as Dex slammed the door, catching her gown in the process. The snick of the lock sounded.

Given that she'd immediately shut her fiancé out, he doubted she cared about anything but escaping.

"Is that bag hers?" he asked the doorman, pointing to the luggage laying on its side.

"Yes."

Dex popped the trunk with the key fob. Then, he looked at the valet. "Put that in the trunk." He slid his hand into the other pocket, retrieving the five-dollar bill he'd stashed earlier. Once the luggage was in the back, Dex slapped the money into his hand.

"What are you doing?" her groom shouted furiously. "You can't take my fiancée anywhere!"

"Move away from the car." Dex glared at the man whose frustrated expression had morphed into anger.

"Who the hell are you?" he asked.

Dex rolled his eyes at the man's stupidity and didn't give him the answer he wanted. "She obviously doesn't want to see you, genius." He strode to his side of the vehicle, unlocking the door and sliding in.

The asshole banged on the passenger side window and Samantha jerked in her seat. "Go!"

Dex put the car in drive and took off, leaving the man yelling at his taillights.

Samantha breathed heavily and twisted the lace on her gown between her hands.

"So, where to?" he asked the distraught woman in the passenger seat.

"I don't know," she said, barely loud enough for him to hear.

He shook his head. "Your apartment?"

"No!" She sucked in a breath. "I mean, that'll be the first place Jeremy will look."

Her phone buzzed in her lap and she clicked off the notification.

He turned a corner and decided driving in large circles until she made a decision was his best bet. "Would you care to tell me what happened to make you run from your wedding?"

She exhaled a deep breath, but her expression was

pained. "I just discovered my fiancé was sleeping with his personal assistant. Not to mention he planned to stay married only long enough for things to look real so he could get half my money. Luckily, I overheard that conversation minutes before walking down the aisle."

He gripped the wheel tighter, wishing he'd throttled the man back at the hotel. What kind of ass set up and cheated on any woman, let alone one as beautiful and smart as Samantha?

"Your brothers are going to kill him," Dex said.

"And then they'll come for me," she muttered.

He raised an eyebrow. "Doubtful. Your family loves you. Speaking of your brothers, does everyone know you left?"

She nodded. "My mom and the bridal party do. Mom told Ian. And I escaped before I had to face him."

Ian was intimidating on a good day but being the oldest brother, he was the de facto patriarch of the family and he'd want to be aware of where his sister went. Ian loved his sisters and he was overprotective of them, so Dex couldn't understand why she thought he would be upset with her. Clearly there was more to this story but asking about it seemed insensitive right now.

Dex glanced toward the passenger seat where Samantha nibbled on her plump bottom lip. He did his best not to groan at the sexy sight. "Look, I get that you're upset, but you need to figure out a plan."

"And I think I have one." She picked up her phone and began to type, finished, and then stared at the screen. Once her phone buzzed again, she smiled.

The same enchanting smile that had caught his attention all those years ago at a New Year's Eve party for the Miami Thunder.

"Yes!" she said with an adorable fist pump. "Take me to Teterboro, if you don't mind," she said of the private airport. "Otherwise, I can call for an Uber. I know you must have come to the hotel for a reason and I hijacked you and your car."

Shit! One look at the gorgeous woman in a wedding dress and he'd forgotten about his meeting with Wes. "Thanks for the reminder." He drove until he saw an empty spot and pulled in, putting the vehicle into park.

"I need to send a message to the friend I was going to meet." He picked up his cell and texted Wes, informing him he wouldn't be there and would explain later, so his pal wouldn't wait any longer than he already had. Then he turned to Samantha. "Why do you want to go to Teterboro?"

"Well, Ian's jet is fueled and ready to go to Turks for my…" She coughed. "Honeymoon." She said the word with great distaste and a scowl. "But I couldn't ask him if I could still use his plane because I know he'd want to have a *conversation* first."

"And you're not ready to deal with your brother," Dex repeated her earlier words.

"Right. But my cousin, Asher, has a jet and a place in the Bahamas and I just asked him if I could spend a couple of days there to regroup." She picked up her phone as if to reaffirm she'd texted him. "And he said of course. So… I need to go to Teterboro."

"Your mom and family will worry."

She shook her head. "I already texted Mom and told her I ran into you, that I was safe and to tell the others. I said I'd let her know where I ended up, so I'll text her from the air."

In other words, she didn't want anyone to stop her.

Dex did his best not to bang his head on his steering wheel as it was only a matter of time before Ian started blowing up *his* phone and asking what the fuck Dex was doing with his sister. It wouldn't be the first time, either.

Dex met Samantha at a New Year's Eve team and family party. He recalled mistletoe and the hottest kiss he'd ever experienced. One that had been so explosive, he'd almost forgotten where they were and why.

And when he'd come up for air, Ian was glaring at

him. With one shake of his head, Samantha's oldest brother and Dex's boss at the time had cut off any possibility of him pursuing the sexy, smart woman he'd been talking to all night. The first female to ever intrigue him with her intelligence and amuse him with her wit. He'd never felt an attraction like it before or since.

But he also knew Samantha wasn't the kind of girl you picked up for a one-night stand, and not just because if he went near her Ian Dare could make his life miserable and his career difficult. Dex hadn't been at the point in his life where a relationship was feasible. He'd been football-focused and hadn't wanted any distractions. He'd had goals and dreams and looking back, he'd accomplished them.

In truth, he wasn't sure how he even thought about the institution of marriage. While Alex and Gloria, his adoptive parents, had a wonderful marriage until her murder—not something he wanted to think about now—his birth parents had spent their lives arguing. Which was why the Sterling house had been his escape.

"Dex? Can you take me to the airport?" she asked again, interrupting his trip into the past and focusing him squarely in the here and now.

He ran a hand through his hair. Could he take her to Teterboro and drop her off to spend however many days alone on an island after such a traumatic experience? Yes to the former… no the latter.

"Want company?" he asked. "Because I'm not dropping you off to be on your own when you're so upset," he said, knowing Samantha was somehow going to change the course of his life.

She looked up at him, through thick lashes and tear-stained makeup. "You'd do that? Fly to the Bahamas at the last minute? We barely know each other. Of course, there was that kiss…" Her cheeks turned pink at the mention of their shared memory.

"There was," he said, wanting her to know he recalled it as well. "But to answer your question, yes, I'd do that for you."

"Then I'd really appreciate it… but can I ask why?"

He let out a pained sigh. "I have a sister and if my friend found Fallon in the same position I discovered you in, I'd hope they'd do the same thing and make sure she was okay."

And keep their hands off his vulnerable sister. Dex would also punch his well-meaning friend once he saw him again just in case he'd had the same wayward thoughts Dex now had about Samantha. And he expected no less of Ian Dare.

But even though Dex would never take advantage of a vulnerable woman, he couldn't deny he'd always wanted a chance with Samantha. That chance just wouldn't be now.

# Chapter Three

DEX SUGGESTED STOPPING by his apartment so he could throw a few things into a suitcase for the trip. Since he was doing her a huge solid by accompanying her, she didn't argue about her need to rush out of town.

His place looked new. It lacked personal touches and some obvious pieces of furniture, and smelled like fresh paint. When she asked, he said he'd just recently moved in and was still furnishing it how he liked.

He directed her to a guestroom where she'd changed into a pair of loose silky pants and a tank top, appropriate for Bahamian weather. She pulled a sweater over her shoulders for the cooler plane ride and left her wedding dress in a heap on his carpeted floor. She never wanted to see the garment again. Being an easygoing guy, Dex hadn't seemed to mind.

Now, on board and in the air, she curled her legs beneath her and looked out the plane window and into the white fluffy clouds. Darkness was falling and seemed apropos considering the mess that was her life.

This morning she'd thought she was getting married and headed to Turks and Caicos on her honeymoon. Now she was in her cousin's plane with a man she'd had a crush on since she'd first seen him on the television screen when watching the Thunder play on Sundays. Then she'd met Dex Sterling in person.

At her brother's New Year's Eve party for his team and their families, she and Dex had shared a long evening of conversation and then a kiss that had ruined her for all other men. Nobody could compete with Dex and the way he'd completely possessed her. With one arm around her waist holding her tight, she'd felt his physical strength against her much smaller frame. And with his talented mouth, he devoured her until her entire body was aroused, even parts she'd never been aware of before.

But no sooner had their lips separated than he'd turned into a different person. Where before the kiss, they'd talked about so many things, after it was like he couldn't get away from her fast enough. She'd taken it as a harsh lesson to her younger self's ego and chalked the incident up to a football player who'd had his New Year's Eve fun and wasn't looking for anything more than a little flirting. Either that, or he thought she was a really bad kisser. But he definitely didn't act like he wasn't enjoying her kiss at the time.

Had she been disappointed things hadn't gone further? Absolutely, because if he'd asked her to go home with him, she'd have said yes in a heartbeat. So she'd taken her bruised self-esteem and gone home to eat a carton of cookie dough ice cream and fall asleep alone. It looked like she'd be doing the same thing tonight, if Maggie, Asher's longtime family housekeeper, kept a flavor Samantha liked in the fridge. Because she was going to need it.

All the while, Dex seemed to understand her need for silence and had left her to her thoughts, while he remained busy with text messages on his phone. Both of their cells hadn't stopped blowing up. Hers with texts from concerned family, friends, and worse, Jeremy, trying to get in touch with her. She frowned at the thought. Not wanting to see his name, she turned her phone off and buried it at the bottom of her bag.

Poor Dex had gotten a phone call from her brother, no doubt, because Samantha wasn't ready to talk to him yet. He'd shot her a pointed look, eyes narrowed, that she interpreted as, *thanks for getting me into this mess,* and rose to take the call in private. She wouldn't avoid Ian forever, just long enough to formulate a reasonable explanation and to fortify herself for the admissions she'd have to give him.

Across from her, Dex had fallen asleep and she envied his relaxed state. All she could think about was how stupid she'd been, ignoring her gut in favor of being stubborn and insisting everything in her life was fine. That mediocre was good enough. That a business plan would lead to a solid, happy marriage.

She plucked her AirPods out of her bag along with her cell, turned to airplane mode so she could continue to shield herself from messages, and settled the white buds in her ears. She set the music to a quality breakup list, mostly courtesy of Taylor Swift, and let herself wallow.

A little while later, movement distracted her. From the corner of her eye, Dex raised his arms over his head, and she realized her companion was awake. She silently took in his full-body stretch, aware of the pull and flex of his muscles beneath the long-sleeve Thunder shirt he'd thrown on along with a faded pair of jeans that hugged his thighs and tight ass. It was all she could do not to let out a girly sigh.

Of course, she reminded herself she'd been on the verge of marrying one man just a few hours ago, she had no right to ogle another guy. No matter how sexy he might be. She flushed with embarrassment and glanced down at the music screen on her phone.

"You can't avoid discussing it forever, you know," Dex said, leaning forward so they could talk.

"I can try." She rubbed her finger over her bottom lip, aware he had a point. "I don't know how to tell my family that they were right. The man I was going to marry, the same man they had a bad feeling about, was using me for my money. That I put all the capital into the business because when I was young and graduating business school, Jeremy talked a good game about how we would conquer the PR world together."

His eyes flashed angry sparks she'd like to think was on her behalf. "You wouldn't be the first person to get duped in a relationship," he said.

"What about the fact that I almost married him without a prenup?"

He'd just lifted a bottle of water to his lips and choked on the sip he'd swallowed.

She slid her gaze from his. "Yep, see? That's why I don't want Ian to know. And before you ask what I was thinking, I'll tell you." She twisted her hands together in her lap. "Jeremy and I met in business school and at the time, all I could think about was having some freedom from my family."

"Sounds like most people in college or grad school."

"Except I was escaping. College was fine, but I went in Florida and my family was close by. I chose grad school in New York and it was a major move. One I really needed."

Leaning back, he crossed one leg over his knee and remained silent, letting her talk and listening, which she appreciated.

"I'm not sure if you know this, but Sienna, my half-sister, had leukemia as a child and needed a bone marrow transplant. My father needed us, his *legitimate* children…" As always, she emphasized the word with quotation marks with her fingers. "…to be tested, and that's how we found out about my father's *other* family. Avery turned out to be the match."

His eyes opened wide. "I knew Ian had a lot of siblings, but I had no idea about the second family or your sister's illness." His expression softened. "That couldn't have been easy," he said in a gruff voice. "Any of it."

"It wasn't." And though it had taken years, all the kids ended up close and Samantha was grateful to have so many brothers and sisters. But it came at a cost. "The illness, almost losing Sienna, it made Ian over-protective of all his sisters, and as my other brothers grew up, they were similarly smothering."

Dex tipped his head to one side, studying her. "I only have one sister but three brothers, and we've all done our best to smother her, too," he said wryly. "Point is, I understand."

"Thank you for that." There weren't many people who would get why she'd made such rash decisions, then doubled down on them.

"So what happened? You met—"

"Jeremy. I met Jeremy and he was a smooth talker and smart. Straight *A*'s and his ideas were intriguing. Soon we were planning to open a PR firm together when we graduated. But he was smooth, as in slick." She curled her fingers into fists. "And I fell for it. Hard. But the business took off, so I thought I'd done the right thing and if he hadn't turned out to be a cheating ass who wanted my money, that would be true."

He pressed his palms against his temples. "I can see why you're worried about Ian's response."

"Thanks." She managed a smile and he laughed, the sound low and pleasurable. "You know, things between Jeremy and I were good in the beginning... but the flame burned out."

At the mention of her romantic past, Dex clenched his jaw. Or maybe she was imagining it. Or maybe his small reaction had nothing to do with her and Jeremy together at all. Just because she sat here spilling her guts, all the while too aware of the man across from her—one she'd once shared a scorching-hot, toe-curling kiss with—didn't mean he felt the same.

"Anyway, the thing is, I'm embarrassed, angry, and... relieved. I shouldn't be relieved he gave me an out... right?"

"You shouldn't be embarrassed, he should. But to answer your question, no, you should not be relieved. Unless... you aren't in love with him?" He phrased it as a question and leaned forward, watching her with interest.

She pulled her bottom lip between her teeth. Was it her imagination or did his eyes darken? One thing she wasn't imagining was her desire for Dex Sterling and it couldn't come at a worse time. She needed to process why she'd been taken in by Jeremy, why she'd ignored her anxiety and many other warning signs and continued with the engagement and wedding... and why she was so focused on Dex and not the man who'd humiliated her moments before walking down the aisle.

But she didn't have time to dwell on any of that, since the pilot announced they were preparing to land. She welcomed the brief reprieve from her confusing thoughts about her ex, and most especially about Dex.

She'd have plenty of time to think about everything while hiding away on the island.

# Chapter Four

DEX WOKE TO the sun shining through his bedroom window and it took a few minutes for him to place where he was. He'd heard about Asher Dare's estate in the Bahamas from Ian and now he was experiencing it firsthand.

Last night, after the private plane had landed, a guy named Corey picked them up from the airport and drove them to the house which had been well-lit for their arrival. The housekeeper was waiting for them and she greeted Samantha with a warm hug and before he knew it, they'd both been offered a bowl of ice cream. Sensing Samantha needed alone time, he'd declined and allowed Corey to lead him to the bedroom where he'd be staying, and he crashed hard.

He braced a hand behind his head and thought back to the conversation he'd had with Samantha on the plane. How sad she'd looked when describing how she'd fallen into a relationship with the bastard who'd set her up and used her for her money. Dex knew a little about that, always being careful not to give the wrong signals to any woman he'd been with. But Samantha was more trusting and Jeremy, the asshole, had taken advantage of her trust.

Dex hoped Ian took care of her SOB ex because if not, Dex wouldn't mind stepping up to protect her. He blinked hard, aware of how out of character that thought had been for any woman who wasn't his sister. He was a lot of things, a playboy being one of them, or so Fallon liked to tell him, but he wasn't someone to take advantage of a hurting woman on the rebound. No matter how attracted he was to her.

Even on the plane, with her eyes red-rimmed from crying, her face makeup-free, and her adorable freckles showing, Samantha had been beautiful. Enough for him to decide to go to sleep instead of sharing ice cream in the kitchen and exchanging more confidences. It didn't help that as he'd turned in for the night, a sobering thought had hit him hard.

Samantha Dare just might be the one that got away.

The harsh ringing of his cell and the sight of Ian Dare's name on the screen jerked him back to reality.

Resigned, he answered the phone. "Morning, Ian."

"Are you ready to tell me what the hell you're doing with my sister?" his former team owner and now friend asked.

Dex rolled his eyes but at the same time, he understood. "I'm taking care of her." He'd already relayed the story of how he'd come across her outside the hotel, omitting the part about almost running her over, when he spoke to Ian yesterday on the plane. But he hadn't given him much else, instead putting him off until now. But he did owe him an explanation. "Something I'd hope you'd do for my sister if the situation were reversed." It never hurt to remind the other man when he was being a pompous jerk. Problem was, Ian liked his reputation as a hardass.

"You know I would take care of your family." Ian paused. "But I want to kill that asshole. I never liked Jeremy Rollins and I told Samantha as much."

"And how'd that go over?" Dex rose from the bed and paced the cold ceramic tile floor.

"Not well. Why do you ask?"

He glanced up at the huge white ceiling fan circling overhead, thinking about the best way to reply. Dex was determined to make things with Samantha's family easier for her.

He hated seeing her so worked up and upset, worrying about what the people she loved would say when they knew the whole story. "Because your sister loves you and knows you're going to freak out. About a lot of things. And as your friend, I'm suggesting you… go easy on her."

"You've known Samantha all of how long? And you're telling me how to deal with my sister?"

Knowing his friend, Dex counted to five in his

head until Ian replied.

"You've got a point."

Dex knew he did. "I'll get her to call you later."

"I'd appreciate that. She's been dodging my calls and texts."

"Because you're leaving her *I told you so* messages!" a female voice called out from Ian's side of the call.

"Hush, baby. Behave, will you?" Ian asked.

Dex chuckled. "I take it that's Riley?" he asked of Ian's wife.

"There's no one else I'd call baby," Ian said in a gruffer voice than before.

"I should hope not," Riley said.

And then Dex thought she whispered something that made him cringe at overhearing their sexual banter. He remembered the days after Ian had met his future spouse. One look and there'd been nobody else for a man who'd never been in a relationship. Had never wanted one. At least Dex wondered whether or not he was cut out for one. There were lonely times at night when he thought about the future and pondered the notion of a family of his own.

Ian cleared his throat. "Back to Samantha. I'm trusting you not to take advantage of my sister when she's vulnerable."

Despite expecting the words, they pissed Dex off anyway and he had to swallow back a *fuck you* retort.

As if Ian didn't know him well enough to have faith in him.

"Don't worry, I know how to treat women, Ian." He let his annoyance show in his clipped tone. "I'll have Samantha call you," he said again, and cut their connection, tossing his phone onto the unmade bed.

Twenty minutes later, he'd unpacked the few things he'd brought with him, showered, dressed in swim trunks, and headed downstairs to see Samantha and find out her plans for the day. And whether or not they included him.

He walked into the kitchen and stopped short. Samantha was already downstairs wearing a white bikini that, as he stared at her curves, took his breath way. She was his ideal woman, her breasts barely more than a handful, her waist indented enough for him to hold, and that ass.

He held back a groan and tore his gaze from her delectable ass cheeks peeking from the bikini bottoms. Instead, he watched her movements. With her hair pulled up in a messy bun and her earbuds in, she flitted around the room singing a Taylor Swift song with words like *begging for forgiveness* belted a little too loudly. Apparently, she was listening to a breakup song. Pausing at the toaster, she shimmied her hips as she pulled out her bagel.

Time to get her attention, he thought, and cleared

his throat. She didn't turn, indicating the volume was turned up loud.

"Samantha?" he called out loudly.

No reply. Just another shimmy while she slathered her bagel with cream cheese.

Before his dick decided to make an appearance, something that would not be happening on this trip or around Samantha at any point in time, he walked up behind her and tapped her on the shoulder.

She shrieked and spun around, those indigo eyes of hers wide with surprise. "You scared me!" She plucked her earbuds out and placed them on the granite countertop.

"Sorry. I called your name but you were busy."

A flush rose to her cheeks. "I was listening to breakup music."

He nodded somberly. "I caught that with some of the lyrics you were singing."

Her blush deepened. "Well, I'm trying to work out my anger." She picked up the bagel and took a bite, her frustration showing with each chew.

"I take it you didn't have a good night's sleep?" he asked.

She shook her head. "Every time I closed my eyes I saw that bastard's face." Tears filled her eyes and his stomach twisted uncomfortably. He hated seeing her this upset.

Evidently, she ate with passion when she was hurting because she took another angry bite of her bagel, leaving cream cheese on her mouth.

Reaching out, he swiped his finger across her bottom lip, capturing the remnants of her breakfast.

Her eyes darkened at his touch and the cock he needed to keep in his bathing shorts twitched, reminding Dex it wasn't happy to be confined. Knowing he was making matters worse, he put his finger in his mouth and licked off the cream cheese.

She let out a soft moan.

"Samantha, honey, you left your phone in the bathroom," Maggie said, walking into the kitchen with a cell in her hand.

"I left it upstairs on purpose."

As if on cue, it rang and Samantha stiffened, then turned back toward the counter.

"I'll take it," Dex said, and Maggie gave Samantha a soft look before handing him the phone. He silenced the device and shoved it into the back pocket of his trunks. "I'll handle things," he whispered to Maggie.

She nodded and quietly left the room.

Dex drew a deep breath and stepped closer to Samantha, placing what he hoped was calming hands on her shoulders and turned her toward him. He expected tear-stained eyes.

Instead, she was laughing, catching him off guard.

"What's going on?" he asked.

"My life is absurd! My family has been giving me the space I asked for… well, all except Ian, but Jeremy? He hasn't stopped leaving messages, phone calls, and texts. As if I believe a) he's sorry, b) I misunderstood what I heard, or c) we can start over again." She shook her head and laughed. "As if… any one of those things were true." Her voice rose to a higher pitch.

Unsure if she was happy, sad, or both, he sighed, knowing this was one of these female moods he wouldn't understand. All he could do was try to keep her mind off yesterday and her ex-fiancé—after he gave her a message from her brother. But he took one look at her face, her mouth parted as if she was about to say something more, and decided Ian could wait.

Samantha came first. "Since you're ready for the beach, how about if we take a walk?"

She raised her eyebrows. "A walk means we might talk some more, and I've had enough. No offense. What if we do something different?" She grabbed something from the chair and slid a short dress over her bathing suit, covering up her luscious body.

"Like what?"

"Parasailing."

He raised an eyebrow. That was the last thing he'd expected her to say but he sensed she still needed to talk. To expunge the poison inside her caused by her ex. "I'll tell you what. I'll go parasailing if you'll take that walk with me later on. A sunset walk."

He'd give her the day to think and process and then see if she needed a shoulder to lean on. It was the least he could do for his friend's sister.

# Chapter Five

THERE WAS NOTHING better than the moment the winch system brought her high in the air and all she could see or think about was the beauty around her. Being four hundred feet above water in a tandem harness, side by side with Dex, floating peacefully in utter silence, allowed for time to put things in perspective. For the next fifteen minutes she could decompress.

Once she landed and heard the ring of a cell phone, or as Dex reminded her of her brother's need to speak with her before they stepped on the boat for their adventure, she'd be forced to reckon with her decisions.

Brandy was handling Samantha's part of the business while she was gone, which enabled her to shake off thoughts of what waited for her on solid ground. Instead, she absorbed the utter beauty of the island and the surrounding water. She stared at the blue ocean below and looked out at the pink sandy shore, and the houses and hotels beyond, appreciating both nature and the pastel man-made structures that dotted the island.

Growing up wealthy, Samantha had always known how fortunate she was to not want for anything. The one time they'd realized money couldn't buy happiness was when they'd found out their father had another family and her half-sister needed compatible bone marrow to live. That was also when she'd learned that life wasn't perfect but if she looked hard enough, sometimes she could find a pot of gold at the end of the rainbow. Samantha was an optimist, it seemed, and after the storm that was her father's destruction of their family, the rainbow came in the form of her new siblings. And the pot of gold was Sienna's recovery, thanks to Avery's generosity.

Hanging on to those memories would be what got her through the fallout of her wedding that hadn't happened, her cheating fiancé, and the fact that she still owned a business with the son of a bitch. She'd survive this because something better was waiting for her on the other side. After she fought through this trauma.

She closed her eyelids and drew a deep breath, letting the warm breeze take her away, the silence and peacefulness making her smile. When she opened her eyes, Dex's powerful body was facing her. He stared right at her and returned her grin, causing her belly to twist in an excitement that had nothing to do with parasailing.

The man was as handsome as they came, with his jet-black hair and light blue gaze hidden from her view by his sunglasses.

Still, when he looked at her, she felt like she was his sole focus. No one else mattered. God, she wished they'd had their chance years ago because now was the epitome of the wrong time to be thinking about any man.

The boat slowed, taking her focus back to the up-coming landing. They were lowered and put into a gentle free fall until her feet and butt dipped in the water. She rose once more, and then the captain finally landed them back in the boat.

"That was amazing," she said, once they'd unbuck-led their harnesses and life vests, returned to shore, and were walking back to the chairs they'd paid for at a nearby hotel.

"Exhilarating," he agreed.

They reached their loungers and he picked up a towel, drying himself off.

Unable to stop herself, her gaze strayed to his bare chest, and the six-pack and muscles he maintained even after leaving football.

"Asher has a gym in the house," she blurted out.

"What was that?"

She shook her head and lowered herself to the seat. No way would she repeat the words and embarrass herself.

A smirk lifted the corners of his mouth, letting her know he'd caught her words, but maybe he just wasn't sure she'd actually said them.

He settled into the lounge chair beside her and stretched out. "So did you get what you needed up there?" He gestured to the sky.

"I did," she murmured. "The peace and quiet gave me time to think."

"And what did you come up with? Any sort of resolution?"

She shook her head and fixed her bun which had strands of hair falling around her face from the wind. "Just that things always work out for the best, but it will take time to learn why things happened the way they did."

"So you're a philosopher type, hmm?"

She shrugged. "Hard lessons learned, that's all."

"I can understand that."

She twisted toward him. "How?" He'd questioned her enough about herself in the last eighteen or so hours. It was time she learned something about him.

His eyes seemed to glaze over and she suspected he was thinking about what he wanted to tell her. And probably what he didn't.

"My biological parents died in a car accident when I was seven." He continued to stare out over the water and she let him, understanding sometimes it was easier to tell a hard story without making eye-to-eye contact.

"I'm so sorry. I had no idea." She couldn't imagine how hard it was to lose both his mother and father at the same time.

Her father had traveled so often, she'd always re-lied more on her mother than her dad, but he'd existed in her life. Once they discovered he hadn't been away on business but with his second family, it was harder to look at him the same way.

"Thanks," he said at last.

A cloud passed overhead, one large enough to know they wouldn't have direct sun for a few minutes, and they both lifted their sunglasses and placed them on top of their heads. She held back the laugh at their synchronized move.

"How'd you end up with the Sterlings?" she asked.

"We lived next door and our families were close. Gloria and Alex took me in and later on, adopted me. They've been my parents longer than my biological ones were." He bent one knee and straightened in the chair so he was now in an upright position. "My point is that if my parents hadn't passed away, I wouldn't be part of the large family I have now and I actually consider myself lucky to be surrounded by them. So I can understand how bad things work out in the end."

She wondered if he missed his real parents. Was

seven old enough to still feel and miss that bond, she wondered but couldn't bring herself to ask? If she and Dex ever got closer, she might learn more about him. But she didn't see that happening. She'd hijacked his life and had no doubt when they left here, he'd distance himself from her all over again. The thought made her sad.

A server walked over, tray in hand. "Can I get you something to drink? Or something to eat?" She held out a plastic menu and Dex took it.

"I'll have a pina colada," she said.

"Corona, please." Dex glanced at the menu and passed it to Samantha. "Want to get lunch?"

She nodded and they ordered burgers and fries.

The rest of the afternoon passed with lighter conversation until Dex's phone rang. He glanced at the screen and groaned.

"Ian?" she asked.

He nodded.

She held out a hand. It was time.

He slid open his phone. "Ian?"

"I thought you said you'd have her call me." Samantha heard Ian's side of the conversation because her brother was speaking *loudly*.

She shook her hand at Dex. "Give it to me."

He groaned and handed her the phone. "I texted you and said I'd call when I was ready," she said to her brother.

"And I haven't slept since you left because I've been worried sick."

She closed her eyes, guilt flooding her. She'd known her brother would be concerned. "I'm sorry. I was just so angry at Jeremy, embarrassed that I had a huge number of people sitting, waiting for a wedding that wasn't going to happen. And I was too mortified to talk to you," she admitted.

"You have no reason to be embarrassed. That jackass is the one who should be too ashamed to show his face in Manhattan," Ian muttered.

"But there's a lot you don't know." She closed her eyes and a tear dripped out. Not because she was sad about losing Jeremy but because she'd been such a fool.

A warm hand came down on her bent knee. She opened her eyes to see Dex had put his hand on her, giving her his comfort, and she drew strength from that.

"Samantha Dare, I want you to listen to me. I can be a bossy pain in the ass, as my wife likes to say, but it's only because I love my family. There is nothing you can tell me that will disappoint me. Or make me turn my back on you."

She sniffed, her tears really flowing now. "You're such a good man. A great brother. And an amazing father."

"Tell that to my daughter who is testing her boundaries with the clothes she thinks it's okay to wear to elementary school. Does she not understand boys get ideas even at that age?"

She was aware that he'd changed the subject for her benefit. "I am sure you're teaching your daughter that if any boy looks at her wrong, to knee him in the balls."

"Ouch," Dex said, squeezing her knee.

"Harsh but true," Ian said.

She managed to smile. "I'm also sure you are telling her she can wear whatever makes her happy and it's on the boy to behave."

He let out a low chuckle. "Damn right. I'm just not ready for her to grow up."

"Well, she's not yet a teen, so relax. You've got time."

Ian snorted. "How did we end up not talking about you?"

"You brought up Rainey, not me. But give my nieces and nephew a kiss for me."

"Speaking of Rainey, she says you owe her another chance to walk down the aisle as a junior bridesmaid."

She'd had her nieces in the wedding party because the girls were so excited and wanted a part in the ceremony. She adored them all but she was closest to

Rainey.

Samantha sighed. "Tell her I'll take it under advisement." But she wasn't signing up for a walk down the aisle anytime soon. She'd been burned enough. "Ian, can a deeper conversation wait for a face to face? I promise you, I'm okay. I just need a few days to process things."

"Sure, Sammy Bean," he said, using his childhood nickname for her that had never made any sense but she liked it anyway. Only he gave her any form of nickname. She'd always been Samantha to everyone else.

"And don't worry. I'm in good hands."

Beside her, Dex groaned loudly.

"There'd better not be any hands on you or I'll meet your plane when you land and show Dex what happens if he touches my sister."

Her eyes opened wide. "Ian Carlton Dare. Stay out of my private life."

That was apparently the wrong thing to say because Dex grabbed his phone back. "Relax, Ian. I'm just here as her sounding board. We need to go now. Lunch is here." Dex disconnected the call without saying goodbye.

"Impressive," she said, as the server handed her a plate with her lunch, then did the same for Dex. Their drinks came next.

"I'm not afraid of your brother, Samantha. I am, however, serious about my food."

They ate in silence, leaving her wondering more about Dex calling himself just her sounding board and bemoaning the fact that she'd never feel those sexy lips on hers again, than about her screwed up life.

A COUPLE OF days later, Samantha sat on the bed wearing a silky robe she'd bought for her honeymoon. Most of her clothes had been purchased with that occasion—and Jeremy—in mind. Pushing that distasteful thought away, she leaned back and thought over her time here in the Bahamas with Dex. A man she preferred thinking about. Especially after seeing how hot he looked in swim trunks, his tanned skin and six-pack mouthwateringly sexy.

Keeping a smart, physical distance from the man she was so attracted to hadn't been easy. Her emotional walls were high. How could they not be after how badly she'd been burned? Though she saw the interest in Dex's eyes, he deserved more than being a rebound guy. Not to mention she'd be putting him in Ian's crosshairs. *She* didn't care what her brother thought about her love life per se, but it wasn't fair to involve Dex when she was all tied up in knots over a marriage that should have happened less than a week ago.

So, since she'd been exhausted after parasailing, she suggested they put off their walk on the beach and Dex had agreed. Instead, she'd had dinner in her room, courtesy of Maggie, before turning in.

Yesterday, she and Dex spent the morning sunning on lounge chairs and after their time on the beach, they walked around town and hit up a restaurant her cousin, Asher, and his wife, Nikki, had recommended. During their time there, she'd purchased necklaces and bracelets for herself, her family, and her best friend.

She'd spoken to Brandy often, mostly, she admitted, to reassure herself someone she trusted had an eye on Jeremy and the business while she was away. Once home, she'd have to face the cheater and his assistant, who she intended to fire. Owning fifty-one percent of the company ought to allow her some perks, she thought. Still, her stomach churned at the thought of seeing the *couple*, feeling a healthy mixture of anger and frustration at Jeremy, at herself, and at everything she'd closed her mind to.

Her cell rang, interrupting her thoughts. A glance told her Jeremy was calling for the umpteenth time and she sent his call directly to voicemail. Then, keeping up with his behavior since she'd tossed the ring his way, he left a voice message followed by a text.

She ignored both. Since they shared a business, she

couldn't block him completely, but she'd rather continue to think about her time on the island with Dex. Their dinner had consisted mostly of her questioning him about his football career and his upcoming job as lead analyst with FSN.

Although Samantha saw the curiosity in Dex's eyes, he humored her by replying and not tossing back some questions of his own. She appreciated him giving her as much information about himself as he had, despite the unfairness of her not offering the same in return.

Time on the island passed quickly and tonight they were going to take that days-ago promised walk on the beach… and she was going to pitch her idea for what she planned as their last night here. It was time to go home and face all she'd left behind.

# Chapter Six

DEX WAS SUPPOSED to meet Samantha at the entrance to the house for their overdue walk on the beach. He was waiting when she walked down the stairs and his breath caught in his throat. A low-cut tank top covered her breasts and a matching white ruffled skirt fluttered around her tanned thighs as she took each step. The visions he had of those long legs wrapped around his waist were nothing short of filthy and his dick hardened in his pants.

She jumped down the final step in a pair of sandals with a small heel. He hoped she planned to take those off for their stroll.

"Hi!" Her smile lit up the room and he saw glimpses of the Samantha he'd first met returning.

"Hi yourself," he said. "Ready for our walk?"

She wrinkled her nose. "I had a better idea. Or rather a bigger idea."

He raised an eyebrow. She'd been doing this since they'd gotten to the island, finding things to keep busy, and he had to wonder if she was pushing the pain down too deep so she didn't need to address everything waiting for her back home. It concerned him that she hadn't broken down in any way that purged the pain of betrayal. At least, not that he'd seen or heard, and her room was next to his.

"Let's hear your idea," he said, wary.

"Well, Maggie is making dinner, so we can take a short walk on the beach by the house, then come back and eat on the deck, and watch the sunset."

So far he was on board. Watching the sunset with Samantha sounded like a damn good idea.

"And after, I thought we'd go to a club in town. I know things are going to be difficult when I get home and I think I've earned a night out dancing. Corey said he'd drive us if you wanted to drink." Her voice raised in excitement, an emotion he wasn't feeling as dancing wasn't on his list of fun activities to do.

He wondered if she was taking this *forgetting her problems thing* too far but she had a point. This was their last night and she did deserve to let go.

She clasped her hands together in a pleading gesture. "Pretty please?"

God, he couldn't deny her anything. "Fine, but I'll drive," he muttered. He didn't need a chauffeur taking them into town and if she planned on drinking, he'd damn well make sure to be sober enough to look out for her.

"Excellent. Come on." Threading her fingers through his, she clasped their hands together and led him through the house, out the back door, and down to the beach below.

She slid off her heels and left them by the lounge chairs and he kicked off his shoes, letting his bare feet curl into the cool sand. To his surprise, she grasped his hand again and walked to the water.

They strolled along the water's edge, enjoying the swath of ocean traveling up the beach and over their feet, then retreating again. He glanced over and caught her profile. She still had a smile on her face and she stopped and looked up at the clouds above.

He'd already experienced the joy in her expression when she'd been parasailing, her issues left on another plane. That was the same woman he'd met years ago and the one he was attracted to now. With the breeze blowing and the sun still in the sky, her skin glowed and it was impossible not to notice how beautiful she was.

"What's wrong?" she asked, obviously catching him staring.

"Not a thing." He tucked a strand of hair behind her ear. "Just admiring the view."

Her cheeks flushed. "It's not so bad from where I'm standing, either."

He liked that answer.

They walked for a little while longer in companionable silence when she stopped. "I think it's time to turn back for dinner."

"Wait." He didn't want to put this off any longer. "You don't have to hold it in, you know."

She wrinkled her nose, her confusion obvious. "Hold what in?"

He huffed out his frustration, knowing he was going to have to spell it out for her. "Even if you're relieved about your wedding not happening, you must have strong feelings about what Jeremy did to you. Holding them in or pretending you aren't feeling them isn't healthy. Now, I may not be one of your girlfriends, but I have a big shoulder you can lean on."

She stared at him, her eyes filling. "I hate him," she said in a shaky voice. "I hate him for manipulating me and my emotions. I resent him for using me, and I'm furious with myself for not seeing him for who he really was. It's not like my family and friends didn't try and tell me."

She attempted to stop the tears with one finger placed in the corner of her eye. "I will not cry over that man."

Though he admired her strength, he hated that she was blaming herself for the asshole's behavior, even if her reaction made perfect sense. "How about turning that anger into something productive?"

She sniffed. "How? And don't make me cry. I don't want to have to redo my makeup."

He swiped a tear that had escaped. "You're gorgeous with or without makeup. I was just going to suggest some planning ahead. What will you do when you have to go back to the office?"

"You mean how will I face Jeremy? That's simple. With my shoulders back and my head held high. I do have fifty-one percent of the business and I want his personal assistant, aka his mistress, gone. I'd love to buy him out, too. I don't want to see his face ever again, but something tells me I'm going to have a fight on my hands."

He clasped both of *her* hands in his. "Something tells me, you can handle it and him."

"Well, I appreciate your faith in me. And I'm okay. I just want to go out tonight and forget about everything because…" She drew a deep breath. "Tomorrow, I think it's time to go home."

Disappointment filled him but despite all the reasons to keep his distance from this intriguing woman, he was glad he'd come. But she was right. Given how well thought out her ideas were, she was ready to leave paradise, so he might as well enjoy the fun-filled night she'd planned.

Their dinner on the veranda was romantic, though neither acted on the intimate atmosphere. Instead, they savored Maggie's blackened grouper, grilled asparagus, and garlic mashed potatoes, while watching the sun set in a blaze of blues, gold, and pink hues.

Samantha told him about her job, the PR accounts she'd won for Dare & Rollins, the company whose name she'd already changed to Dare PR, at least in her mind. She'd obviously put her heart and soul into the business and he knew she'd fight Jeremy to the bitter end to keep the career she'd built.

After the delicious meal, Dex drove them into town and found a parking space on the street, maneuvering the vehicle easily despite being on the opposite side of the road from what he was used to.

There was one club in town and tonight's theme offered a futuristic neon party. Together, they walked into the bar and techno music filled the room. Bright colors flashed around him, altering quickly enough to give him a splitting headache. If Dex needed proof his barhopping days were behind him, this setting was it.

Samantha, on the other hand, was having the time of her life. While he refrained from drinking, she'd gone all in. Coming off the bottle of wine they'd shared at dinner, she was enjoying a fruity cocktail. He'd made sure to watch the bartender mix her drink each time she ordered another.

He found a small table close to the dance floor. They started out watching the other patrons but eventually, she made her way into the crowd, immediately meeting a bunch of women her age celebrating a bachelorette party, and they took her into their group. He, on the other hand, remained at a table near the parquet dance floor, attempting to keep an eye on her through the flashing fluorescent lights and the movement around her. Watching her sway to the music wasn't a hardship and he leaned back, nursing a beer.

After a while, Samantha sashayed over to him and braced her hands on his shoulders. "Come dance with me," she said loudly, asking for the umpteenth time.

"I'll tell you what." He, too, raised his voice to be heard over the music. He clasped his hands on her waist and reminded himself she was drunk and he was a gentleman.

"What?" Her pretty navy eyes sparkled with amusement.

"I will dance…" he began.

"Oooh good!" She clapped her hands, reminding him of her intoxicated state.

"But not until they play slow music and stop flashing those damned distracting lights." Which meant, he wouldn't be getting on the dance floor this evening. No matter how much he wanted to feel her curvy body against his, the beat, the lights, and the atmosphere weren't his thing.

She bent low, giving him a perfect view down her cleavage inside her top. Soft mounds of tanned flesh teased him and he groaned, aware nobody would hear him over the music.

Forcing himself to look up, he met her gaze, those heavy-lidded eyes locking on his lips. His dick reacted, thickening in his pants with one goal in mind. Not happening, he reminded himself.

"I bet I can convince you," Samantha said, her mouth way too close.

Before he could react, soft and eager lips met his. This woman had starred in his dreams since their first kiss. It had been easier to tell himself he'd put their interlude behind him when there was no chance of them being together. Now, he grasped onto this one kiss because *one* was all it could be. She was too drunk to know what she really wanted and on the rebound from her jerk ex.

But a kiss she'd remember in the morning? That, he could give her. Swiping his tongue over her lips, he caught a tangy hint of cranberry along with the vodka in her spritzer but he got a bigger taste of Samantha.

He clamped his hand behind her neck, holding her in place as he took over, gliding his tongue against hers. She moaned, the sound reverberating through him, and suddenly the lights and irritating sounds faded into the background. All he could focus on was Samantha, her plush lips and delectable taste, and his body thrummed with a need that wouldn't be satisfied tonight.

But he wasn't thinking about himself. Why would he when Samantha had lowered herself onto his lap, her breasts pressed into his chest? She rocked against his hard cock and he swallowed a curse. *This* was not happening here. In fact, this wasn't happening at all, no matter how much he wished otherwise.

He removed his hand from behind her neck, giving her hair a tug, and receiving a shuddering moan into his mouth in return. Instead of slipping his hand beneath her skirt and gliding his fingers over her wet pussy the way he wanted to, he cupped her face between his hands and ended their kiss.

Her eyes were glazed with the same desire that flared inside him but he couldn't do anything about it in a room full of people. Not with this woman. Before he could explain why he'd stopped, someone called her name.

They both looked as the group of bachelorette party women made their way toward them.

"Sam, come dance!" one of them yelled over the music.

Sam? He didn't have to mull over the nickname to know a man's version of her name didn't suit her. Elegant and unique, she was Samantha.

She looked over her shoulder at the women, then back at him, obviously torn. Probably because her new friends didn't appear to be leaving without taking her with them to the dance floor.

He slid his finger over her damp bottom lip. "Go. Have fun. I'll be right here waiting."

She waltzed off, hips swaying, and with his dick hard, he settled in to watch her.

An hour later, he'd decided they'd both had enough. Getting her to leave was no easy feat, so he scooped her into his arms and carried her out as she waved to her new friends and promised to keep in touch.

# Chapter Seven

THE NEXT MORNING, Samantha nestled into the plush seat on the jet with the hangover of all hangovers. Her head pounded and her mouth tasted like cotton, reminding her of the nights she overdid it in college. She'd had some embarrassing moments back then, but none came close to what she'd done with Dex last night.

After he'd been gracious enough to rescue her from humiliation and had taken time off to accompany her to the Bahamas, how did she repay him? By kissing and mauling the man. She could still feel the hard ridge of his erection over her swollen, needy sex, desire pulsing through her as if her panties hadn't existed.

She groaned and adjusted her sunglasses which she still wore on the plane. She'd already closed the window shades, the glare of even the clouds making her migraine worse.

"Are you feeling sick?" Dex asked from his seat beside her.

They hadn't spoken much since they'd met up out front so Corey could load the car.

"No." She shook her head and immediately regretted the motion. If she did that again, the answer to his question might become yes. She kept her eyes closed until the flight attendant walked over and offered them drinks.

Forcing a smile at the man, she replied, "A large glass of water, please." If Samantha knew Asher, she'd soon be drinking a high-end brand. She shut her eyes again, still not ready to face Dex.

"Orange juice, if you have some," he said. Probably because it was still early in the morning and he wasn't nursing the hangover from hell, needing hydration desperately.

When she'd arranged for the jet to leave early this morning, getting as drunk as she had had not been on the agenda. But Dex made it so easy for her to let go and free her emotions. When they'd walked on the beach, she'd expressed her pain and anger, and he'd offered her a shoulder to lean on, making her feel like a priority in a way Jeremy hadn't in years. If ever.

Knowing that Dex was watching her at the club gave her the safety to drink and enjoy herself. Then she'd met Katie, the bride, who was a New Yorker like herself, along with her entourage. The rest of the night was a little fuzzy but not enough that she didn't remember trying to coax Dex to dance. She recalled his amusement. How sexy he looked in a pair of black slacks and white T-shirt that showed off his muscular, tanned skin. How delicious his musky cologne had smelled.

Then, thanks to alcohol-induced bravery, she'd kissed him.

And instead of pushing her away, holy hell, had he kissed her back. The entire interlude lasted just a few minutes but it was enough to remind her that she hadn't experienced such passion in a long time.

Damn, she hadn't had *sex* in a long time, either. Jeremy had always claimed they were too tired after a long day at work. *They.* As if he knew what she wanted… or didn't want in bed. Now Samantha knew the truth. Jeremy had been getting his satisfaction elsewhere. She inwardly cringed at how stupid she'd been. How she'd allowed him to gaslight her in so many areas of her life.

She could try and convince herself that her sexual slump was the reason her body had melted for Dex, but she knew it would be a lie. Their chemistry had only grown stronger over the years, the kiss so explosive she was lucky she hadn't come in public.

She wasn't a virgin nor was she a prude. Though she hadn't been overly experienced prior to meeting Jeremy, she'd had lovers, been kissed, been curious and tried out various positions with men she wasn't in a serious relationship with. But she'd *never* experienced such overwhelming need after a simple lip-lock before.

But there was nothing simple about Dex Sterling.

He'd broken their kiss first and hadn't tried anything when they'd returned to the house. Of course, that could be because he'd had to carry her out of the club while she waved like a pageant winner.

God, she was never going to live this down. The best thing she could do was open her eyes and get it over with. She pivoted in her seat and pulled off the polarized dark lenses, only to find him watching her.

An apology would go a long way toward making her comfortable with him again. She hoped. *Do it,* she instructed herself. *Just say what you're thinking.* "I'm sorry I kissed you at the bar last night."

His lips pulled into that sexy smirk she loved. "I'm not."

She blinked in surprise. He couldn't possibly mean it the way it sounded. Like he'd wanted to kiss her, too.

"Well, that's nice of you to say but I know you're just trying to make me feel less mortified over my behavior last night. I didn't plan on getting so toasted. I mean, I haven't been drunk like that since college." She gripped the armrests tighter with both hands, needing the support to get through this apology.

She felt, rather than saw, him turn toward her, and when she still stared forward, he put his knuckles beneath her chin and encouraged her to meet his gaze.

"Everyone needs to let loose sometimes. Which reminds me.

Last night, the girls called you Sam. Did you like the nickname?"

She shook her head and groaned. Some people had nicknames that worked. She'd never been a Sam. "Why do you ask?"

"Because a woman like you deserves a special nickname." A more serious expression took hold and his eyes turned a touch darker than earlier. "I think I'll stick with Samantha."

He spoke like they'd be spending time together after they landed and her stomach swished in a good way. One that had nothing to do with her hangover and a lot to do with how he made her feel.

"I don't understand. *You* stopped the kiss." And he hadn't stayed with her last night, though she had a vague recollection of asking him to. And that invitation was something she refused to dwell on. It was too mortifying on top of already being embarrassed, she thought.

"Samantha," he said, this time in a gravelly voice that caused bigger flutters in her belly. "I stopped because you were in no condition for me to take advantage of you. No matter how much I wanted to."

He wouldn't have been taking advantage but she understood what he meant. She bought the too drunk excuse. Dex was a gentleman.

Still… "This is the second time you walked away from kissing me." And she didn't say that as a *poor me* type of thing, either. She was just stating a fact.

He clenched his strong jaw and she had no idea what was going on behind those light blue eyes. "One day, we will have a long overdue talk. But for now—"

Before he could finish, the pilot's voice came over the intercom. "We are starting our descent into Teterboro and there's heavy rain. I expect turbulence, so please check that your seat belts are fastened. We should be on the ground in about thirty minutes."

The flight attendant walked over and removed their drinks.

A few seconds later, they hit the rough air, and the plane began to bounce, at least that's what it felt like. Instinct had her grabbing for Dex's arm and gripping tight. Normally she could handle turbulence, but not when she was suffering from a pounding headache and nausea from overindulging.

He placed his strong palm over hers and spoke comforting words about how the bumps and dips would end soon. When she dug her nails into his skin, he changed the subject to a funny story about how after a game, their running back had been hit in the face with a shaving cream pie by a teammate, *while* he was talking to the media.

She laughed. "Did he have a sense of humor?"

"Not much," Dex said, chuckling. "Now you tell me a story."

The plane jolted again and she let out a moan, leaning her head on his forearm.

"Story, remember?" he asked, rubbing her back.

"Right." She kept her head on his arm and thought back to her childhood. His shaving cream story sparked the memory of one Halloween. "So instead of trick-or-treating, my siblings and I took shaving cream from the bathroom and had a foam fight." She couldn't stop smiling as she recalled that fun night. "Then, we went home and rang the doorbell. Ian answered, dressed in his good clothes, as always."

"No big shock," he said laughing. "And I see where this is going," he said, his smile still wide.

She nodded. "Well, we couldn't leave him so clean and proper, so we attacked him, tackling him until he was covered in foam like the rest of us. He didn't speak to any of us for a full week."

Dex let out a loud laugh. "That's amazing. I've never seen Ian dressed in anything but a suit and tie."

"As a teen, he was always dressed like a man. Sweaters and pressed pants."

Laughter filled the cabin and she thought Dex had the best laugh.

Before she knew it, they were landing and the turbulence was behind her. She even felt better once they were on terra firma except, she realized, it was time to say goodbye.

They stood on the runway under umbrellas and waited for someone to deliver their bags from the plane. Once they had them, they rolled them into the main area where people congregated before their private flights.

"Can I give you a lift home?" Dex asked. He'd parked his car in the long-term lot the day they left for the Bahamas.

She shook her head. "I thought I'd take an Uber to Brandy's apartment. I'll stay there tonight and deal with Jeremy living in my place tomorrow.

"No need to take an Uber when I have my car. Where does Brandy live?"

She was about to answer when she caught sight of a man with her name on a sign. "Apparently, someone in my family sent a driver." She waved at the man and he made his way over.

"I see," Dex said.

Did he sound disappointed or had he offered the ride out of obligation and was relieved to be rid of her? It hadn't slipped her mind that the turbulence had ended their serious conversation about him being the one to end their two kisses. For that she was grateful.

"I'm sure we both know who sent the driver. Since

Asher is aware of the flight plan, he probably called Ian."

Silence descended and their eyes locked, the tension between them palpable. This was going to be an awkward goodbye unless she took charge.

"Thank you," she said softly.

His brows drew together. "For?"

He'd let his facial hair grow in on the island and he was so damn sexy with the beard. She wondered if he'd keep it and realized she'd probably find out when she turned on the sports network for a football game. The thought of not seeing him again made her sad.

"For not hitting me with your car?" She forced out a laugh. "No, seriously. For picking up a runaway bride and taking her far away from her disastrous non-wedding."

She felt his smile in her belly… and lower.

"I can honestly say it was my pleasure." His gruff voice didn't help the spinning in her stomach that had everything to do with Dex.

Reaching out, she clasped his hand in hers. "You're a stand-up guy, Dex Sterling. Thanks again." She stepped closer, rose onto her tiptoes, and pressed a long kiss on his cheek, lingering because she wasn't ready to part ways and he smelled so good.

His hands rested on her waist. "And you're someone worth knowing, Samantha Dare. Don't ever settle.

You deserve a man worthy of you. Someone who will give you the world on a silver platter."

She smiled sadly because that man wouldn't be him.

# Chapter Eight

AFTER LEAVING SAMANTHA in the hands of the driver her brother had sent, Dex texted his parents and siblings to let them know he was home. They were such a big group, the family chat made sure he didn't leave anyone out. Remy had suggested they come to his bar for dinner and everyone agreed. The timing gave Dex a chance to go home for some much-needed processing, considering he'd left for the Bahamas on such short notice.

While there, he showered, changed, and even hung up Samantha's wedding dress in a spare closet. In case she decided she wanted the garment one day. Though he didn't like thinking of her wearing a wedding gown for another man. And that thought shook him up more than he cared to admit.

Later, he was the first to arrive at The Back Door, if he didn't count Remy, who owned the place, and said hello to the staff he knew well before sitting down at the table reserved for the family. Soon, everyone joined him and their loud meal began.

They'd finished dinner and dessert, and no one seemed in any rush to separate and head home. Banter and chatter went on around him but Dex couldn't concentrate on anything but thinking about Samantha. How was she doing now that she was back in New York? How would she handle the douchebag who'd used her? Personally, Dex would like to wring his neck for making her cry and embarrassing her in front of the people who mattered to her.

Dex had no doubt he'd be hearing from her brother for his opinion. Not that Dex would tell Ian anything about Samantha that felt private. Ian might be his friend, but he couldn't help but feel his loyalty was to Samantha.

"Earth to Dex. Where are you?" Remy asked from the seat beside him.

"Still in the Bahamas with his ex-boss's sister," Fallon said, a teasing glint in her eyes.

"Why didn't you bring your bride to meet us?" Remy asked.

"Behave!" Raven, Remy's wife, said. They'd gotten engaged six months ago and married a short month later. The event included the Sterlings, a few people from work, including Zach Dare and his wife, Hadley, Raven's brother, and Caleb and his son, Owen—the only family Raven acknowledged. She'd been through hell, come out the other side, and didn't want to look back.

Dex glanced at Remy and rolled his eyes. "You

know the real story about how I ended up in the Bahamas with Samantha, so cut it out."

But a part of him wondered how Samantha would get along with his rowdy group of relatives. Knowing she'd come from an even larger group of siblings, she'd probably fit in fine, then he'd reminded himself there was no reason to give that question any thought.

"How is she?" Lizzie, their former housekeeper, and now his father's girlfriend, asked. "It can't be easy to find out the man you're about to marry was using you for your money."

Dex groaned. "She held it together pretty well on the island but I think now that she's home and has to face him and untangle their lives, things might hit her harder."

"Poor thing," Lizzie murmured softly.

She had been a mother to them all once they moved to the house where she lived in the guesthouse on the property. Her husband had died of a heart attack and when the owner sold it to Alex, he'd made it a condition that he allow Lizzie and her daughter, Brooklyn, to continue to live there. Since their mom had been killed a few years before, Lizzie had taken them all into her heart.

Conversation picked up around them; his brothers, Jared and Aiden, discussing business, while his father turned to Lizzie, leaving Fallon and Dex to their own discussion.

"How's the gallery doing?" he asked his sister.

"Great! I had a showing for a new artist this past weekend and we had a good amount of orders." Her eyes sparkled with excitement. As much as she loved painting, she adored discovering new talent. "But I'm curious about Samantha Dare. It's crazy how you ran into her outside the hotel. You knew her through Ian?"

He nodded, deciding his sister did not need to know about their past New Year's Eve kiss. "I recognized her. She knew me and begged me to get her out of there."

"So you played white knight."

He shrugged his shoulder. "I just helped her out." He was about to say anyone would have done the same but when he thought about the lengths to which he'd gone… he kept his mouth shut.

"It was nice of you, Dex. I mean, I know you and Ian are friends, now that he's not your team owner, but still. That was above and beyond."

He and Ian had developed more of a mentor-mentee relationship in the earlier years of him joining the Thunder, but once Dex reached star status, he felt like Ian's equal. Their relationship turned into more of a friendship, and continued to this day, which was why the situation with Samantha had always been complicatcd.

"Is she pretty?" Fallon nudged him with her elbow.

"Who?"

His sister laughed. "The woman you're thinking about when you aren't paying attention to what's going on around you."

There was no point in lying. "She's beautiful." Those unique-colored eyes, the freckles that came out in the sun...

"Ooh and are you interested in her?" Fallon propped her chin in her hand and stared him down.

"Sometimes I think I am." Okay, *that* was a whopper. He'd always been interested in Samantha. "But I won't be anyone's rebound."

She nodded. "Understandable. But I know you and you're charming when you put your mind to it." She grinned at him and laughed. "I'm joking. You're always a charmer. But all those reasons you didn't get involved with women while focusing on football are gone now."

"What does me being charming have to do with retirement from football?"

"Focus!" She snapped her fingers in the air. "I'm saying if you're so attracted to Samantha Dare, put your mind to being more than her rebound. Be the man of her dreams."

"Even if I thought that was a good idea, I'm going

to be traveling a lot for the new job," he reminded her.

She shook her head at him. "Not until September. That gives you plenty of time. What else?"

Persistent little thing, he thought wryly. "Any time I ask myself if I'm ready to give a relationship a try, my early years with my biological parents come back to me." In vivid living color. "The fighting, the screaming." He shook his head. "I'm not sure I trust a long-term thing not to turn into a negative experience."

But did he really see himself fighting with any woman the way his parents had? Fuck, no. And he couldn't imagine Samantha raising her voice in anger, except at her douchebag ex, but not for bullshit like dishes in the sink.

His parents had been dysfunctional. Before their deaths, they'd been a combustible couple. The sound-track to his youth had been their arguments. He'd overheard the police tell Alex that a witness said he'd seen the female passenger, Dex's mother, reach for the steering wheel before the driver lost control of the vehicle. Dex had never mentioned anything to Alex or Gloria but he had no doubt his biological parents had been in one of their rip-roaring arguments prior to the crash. But he'd run back to Remy's room before he could hear more.

Fallon slung one arm over his shoulders. "Dad and Mom got along really well. I know you remember that."

"And Dad nearly fell apart after her death. We lived with Nana and Pops for a long time until Dad was ready to handle life again and bought the house."

"Because he felt guilty that one of his clients was angry that Dad had lost money managing his accounts, and he went after Mom in retribution." Fallon swallowed hard, picked up a napkin, and dabbed at her eyes. "Life happens, Dex. Nobody knows that better than you. But are you really going to use your biological parents Derek and Sherry's issues as an excuse not to live a full life?"

He didn't know what he thought except he couldn't get Samantha out of his mind.

"Fallon?" Brooklyn, Lizzie's daughter, called to get her attention. The two were like sisters.

"Promise me you'll think about what I said?" Fallon asked him.

He nodded and she turned to answer her friend, leaving Dex with his thoughts about his time on the island. Last night in the Bahamas, after bringing Samantha home from the club, he'd helped her out of the car and when she tripped on the stairs, he lifted her into his arms again and carried her to bed. He laid her down, watching her curl up, still in her dress because he was determined to be a gentleman, and fall asleep.

But not before she'd mumbled, asking him to stay. The desire to wrap his arms around her while she slept had been strong, which was why he'd escaped to his bedroom as soon as possible. Memories of that sizzling kiss had tortured him all night long.

But staying away had been the right thing to do. And that shouldn't change. He had too much going on in his life to involve himself in Samantha's. Not to mention the Ian issue. Even if he wished otherwise.

WHEN THE DRIVER at the airport asked where Samantha wanted to go, she'd immediately said Brandy's apartment. Since Samantha had no idea if Jeremy was still living in her place, the one he'd moved into, she'd opted for her friend's. She'd face her ex-fiancé tomorrow, once she had a good night's sleep and a clear head. She'd spent the day at Brandy's and her friend had taken the afternoon off work to hang out with her.

Later that night, Samantha curled up in the corner of Brandy's sofa, a pint of ice cream in one hand and a tablespoon in the other. If she kept up the junk eating, she'd have trouble fitting into her clothes.

"Thanks for letting me stay over," she said.

Brandy was digging into her own pint of chocolate

ice cream. "Don't be silly. Stay as long as you want."

"And I appreciate you holding down the fort at work while I was gone." She didn't know what she'd do without the one friend she knew she could trust.

"How about you stop thanking me for doing things I know you'd do for me, and tell me about your trip with the hottie quarterback," Brandy said.

"Retired quarterback. Starting in September, he's going to be the lead analyst for *Sunday Night Football.*" And Samantha was proud of him. It hurt that the only place she might see him from now on was on the television screen.

"Which means you have a good amount of time to spend with him before he begins his traveling to the games for work."

Brandy sounded much too positive considering the state of Samantha's life and she shook her head. "Dex did me a favor by coming to the Bahamas, but our time together is over. I have to figure out how to handle Jeremy, not a new man. Besides, I doubt I'll be hearing from Dex again." The thought settled like lead in her stomach.

"You don't see the interested sparkle in your eyes that I do when you talk about Dex." Brandy put her empty container on the coffee table, but held on to the spoon and sat back, leveling it at Samantha and using the utensil to make her point. "But I'll let you live with your delusions for a little while longer." She swung her feet over the edge of the sofa and rose to her feet. "Let me toss the empty containers." She gathered up the trash and walked to the kitchen, returning with two bottles of water, handing one to Samantha.

"Thanks."

"You're welcome. So, what's your plan regarding Jeremy?" Brandy asked, settling back into her chair.

Samantha laid her head back, closed her eyes, and groaned. Then she opened her eyelids and met her friend's gaze, determined to stop with the *poor me* routine. Even if it was just inside her head. "Tomorrow I'll show up at the office and let it be known I'm back, I'm fine, and I'm in charge."

Brandy grinned. "Damn right. Nobody gets my girl down. What about your living situation? The apartment is yours. It's not right that he's still there."

Once Samantha had been settled at Brandy's, she'd called her doorman and asked that very question. Apparently, Jeremy had no shame because he hadn't moved out.

"You're right. It's mine and I want him out. My name is on the lease. If Jeremy shows up at the office tomorrow, I'll head home and have the locks changed. Let the bastard find somewhere else to live."

"And she's back." Brandy clapped her hands in approval. "You know I'll support you, right?"

Samantha's eyes watered at her friend's loyalty. "I know, and I am so grateful to have you in my corner."

"Is it awful how much I'm going to enjoy watching you take back what's yours?" Brandy asked.

Samantha couldn't help but laugh. "No. I'm well aware I didn't listen to your warnings about Jeremy either." By then, she'd been in too deep.

Curling her legs beneath her, Brandy shifted until she was comfortable. "I just knew you could do better. And he thinks way too highly of himself."

"I can see that now," Samantha whispered.

Brandy let out a sigh. "Don't be hard on yourself. You aren't the first woman to fall for a snake's charm."

"Well, I'm finished with this particular snake. I plan to get the best lawyer I can, so I'm going to call Ian tomorrow. I need the name of a shark." To reclaim her business and her life.

"Did your family go home to Florida after... after Sunday?" Brandy asked, obviously tiptoeing around the words *aborted wedding*.

Samantha nodded. "Mom's back home. So are my brothers and sisters," she said, thinking of her half-siblings, too. "But Ian came back to New York to meet with some investors and to talk to me."

"Did I mention that your brother intimidates the hell out of me? And not many people do."

Samantha grinned. "It's his M.O. But if you want to see his softer side, check out how he is with his wife and kids." Thinking of her nieces and nephews always warmed her heart.

"I know, and I was kidding. Sort of. He'd do anything for you."

She nodded in agreement. Though she wasn't thrilled with the prospect of their conversation, she'd feel better getting the entire story of her business deal with Jeremy off her chest. Ian wouldn't be happy but he'd help her no matter what.

"Tomorrow is going to be a long, hard day. I think it's time to turn in for the night." Samantha rose to her feet and Brandy did the same.

"Good night and welcome home," her friend said. "Let me know if you need anything." Brandy strode over and pulled Samantha into a hug. "Sleep well."

She'd need to if she was going to be on her A game tomorrow when dealing with her employees and her ex-fiancé.

# Chapter Nine

SAMANTHA ARRIVED EARLY at work. Never mind that she'd had to borrow clothes from Brandy, she was here, coffee in hand, ready to face the day and her ex. Leaving her latte on her desk, she strode out of her office and Brandy winked as she passed.

"Good luck, Tiger."

Rolling her eyes at her friend's humor, Samantha kept walking. By coincidence or design, and she was beginning to think the latter, Jeremy's space was on the other end of the floor they occupied.

Ignoring the stares, she concentrated on the click of her slightly too small, borrowed heels as she made her way to her destination. She approached Jeremy's assistant/fuck buddy's desk.

Marley smartly remained in her chair and even slunk down in her seat.

Samantha rapped twice on the door and let herself in without waiting for an invitation, slamming the door behind her.

"Samantha!" Jeremy jumped up from his desk.

She took one look at his tall, lean physique, slicked-back hair and arrogant expression, and wondered what she'd ever seen in the man. Worse, she found herself comparing him to Dex, the former pro-football player with broad shoulders and muscular arms, a six-pack, and an Adonis belt that made her swoon. But what she found most endearing about Dex was his warm, charming personality and protective nature, all things Jeremy lacked. Too bad she hadn't realized it sooner.

"You're back!" he exclaimed.

"Obviously," she said, gritting her teeth.

"I'm glad because we really need to talk." He walked around his desk, making his way toward her, and she stiffened, not wanting him near. Maybe he'd sensed her resistance because he paused a decent distance away. "I've tried to reach you but you wouldn't take my calls. Darling, I'm so sorry. Marley was a mistake and it will never happen again." Though he sounded contrite, she wasn't fooled nor was she stupid.

Her eyes were open now, both to his betrayal and her own complicit behavior in ignoring the signs and warnings given to her by friends, family, and Jeremy himself. He glanced at her face, his gaze penetrating hers, obviously looking for an *in* somewhere. When he didn't find one, his shoulders drooped.

Now, it was her turn. "You're right. It won't hap-pen again because I no longer want anything to do with you."

He paled beneath his tanned skin. "You don't mean that. All couples go through ups and downs. We can fix things." He reached for her hands and she took a step back.

The arrogant prick. Did he really think she'd accept his cheating and planning to steal her money? He'd obviously forgotten *that* part of his conversation with Marley. Though she'd love to throw the reminder in his face, she took Ian's words to heart. He'd texted her this morning, warning her not to discuss business with Jeremy, or her plans regarding their partnership until she'd spoken to a lawyer.

"You'd be amazed what time away from you did for me. I've done some reflecting and the fact is, the life we shared isn't the life I want to live." Spending time with a sexy, confident, attentive man like Dex had pointed out all that was missing in their relationship.

Jeremy's lips pulled in a firm line. That was his tell. She was aggravating him. Good, she mused, unable to control her smile. It was time the tables turned.

"You're just hurt and upset," he said, clearly gearing up to try and sway her again. "But I'll convince you we're meant to be."

Ignoring that piece of stupidity, she focused on what was important. "We're partners in the business, so I want to set some ground rules for work."

His gaze narrowed. "Go on."

"I want Marley gone." Not only couldn't she look at the other woman but she didn't trust her with any Dare and Rollins business. Not even as Jeremy's assistant. Besides, taking away his toy would give Samantha immense pleasure.

"Done," he said immediately. "I told you I want us to work and I'll do whatever I have to, to make that happen. Just tell me what else I can do."

That was the easiest question yet. "Get out of my apartment."

He flinched as if she'd slapped him. "You don't mean that."

"I do." She straightened her shoulders. "We're over and I'm going to make sure you understand that." She turned toward the door and paused. "Do your best to stay out of my way at work, too. I don't want to see you any more than necessary."

Without waiting for an answer, she let herself out of the room, only to find Brandy waiting for her a few steps away from Marley's desk. The other woman had disappeared.

"Did you scare off the witch?" Samantha asked, as they walked back to her office.

Brandy let out an evil laugh. "I glared until she mumbled something about a coffee break and scurried away like the mouse she is. How'd it go?"

Samantha waited until they were back in her private office with the door closed. "He groveled and I made myself clear. It's over between us and Marley is gone."

"He agreed to that?" Brandy asked, sounding surprised.

Samantha walked around to her desk and began to gather her purse, laptop, and a few other things. "He actually thinks he can win me back, the delusional asshole." Drawing deep breaths into her lungs, she waited until she calmed down and as her heart rate slowed, her anger grew. "I hate him for what he did to me."

"He's not worth the expended energy," Brandy said in a soothing voice.

"Maybe not but I'm not finished fixing my life." She reached for her phone inside her bag, pulled up Ian's contact details, and dialed her brother's number. "Ian? Can you meet me at my apartment?"

"Whatever you need," her brother said.

"Thank you. I'm leaving the office now." She disconnected the call and glanced at her friend.

Brandy grinned. "Go home, talk to Ian. You two work out a plan to kick Jeremy's ass. Just make sure I have a front-row seat when you do."

Samantha laughed. "You're a good friend."

"The best," Brandy agreed. "Don't worry about

anything. I'll handle things here."

Samantha gave her friend a grateful hug, picked up her bag, and walked out of her office, plan in mind. She was Samantha Dare and her slimeball ex-fiancé would not get the better of her. No way, no how.

DEX SAT ON a barstool at The Back Door. He'd arrived around noon and talked to Remy until he'd been called into the kitchen. It was twelve-thirty and he was now on his second beer. This one he planned to nurse until he'd figured out what the fuck to do about the woman he couldn't get out of his head.

"Hello, big brother." Fallon slid into the stool next to him, taking him by surprise.

"Shouldn't you be at the gallery?" he asked.

She nodded. "But rumor has it you need a female perspective on life, so I'm here to give it to you."

"Remy," he muttered. "That's what I get for spilling my guts." Something he was not used to doing, but apparently when Samantha burrowed her way in, she was impossible to get out and he'd needed advice. Remy told him to go for it, which wasn't much help analyzing, something he liked to do.

She laughed, then placed her elbow on the bar and her chin in her hand. "No, that's what you get for having siblings. So, you can't stop thinking about Samantha."

"I'm worried about her." He told himself thinking about her nonstop and being worried about her well-being was a whole different animal. "She has to face her bastard fiancé for the first time and I'm just concerned."

"So much so that you're here, sulking over a woman you can't stop thinking about."

He opened his mouth and she held up her hand.

"A woman you're concerned about." She shifted on the stool, adjusting the long flowing skirt she wore. "Which begs the obvious question, if you're so worried about her, why don't you just go see her and find out for yourself how she's doing?

"We had this conversation and I told you to turn on the charm and work your way out of the rebound thing, but now I'm going to adjust. Get your ass over there and check on the woman. Settle your mind. She'll see you're a good guy but that's not the purpose of the visit. Those things are secondary benefits." His sister stared at him, her lips lifted as she tried not to laugh.

He decided to humor her. "And what, may I ask, is the primary benefit?"

She lifted her hand and flicked his head with her thumb and forefinger.

"Ouch! What was that for?" He rubbed the side of his head where it stung.

"Stop driving yourself crazy and go see her. I guarantee the second you look at her, you'll know whether or not you're in."

He was in, all right. Way over his head.

"Thanks, sis." Leaning over, he kissed her cheek. "If I haven't said it lately, I appreciate you."

She smiled. "And you can show me by buying me lunch."

Once they finished, he walked Fallon out to her Uber and dialed Samantha to find out where she was and when they could meet. Her phone went direct to voicemail.

Now that he'd made the decision to see her, he didn't want to wait. A quick Google check and he called her office, using the directory dial to reach her.

"Hello? Samantha Dare's office. Brandy Bloom speaking."

He recognized her name as Samantha's PA. "Is Samantha in?"

"I'm sorry. She can't come to the phone. Who may I say is calling?"

"It's Dex Sterling."

"Dex!" Brandy said, as if they were best friends. "Samantha left for the day. Did you try her cell phone?" she asked.

"It went to voicemail. Can I leave a message?"

A few seconds of silence followed before Brandy answered. "She actually went home for the day. I'm sure she wouldn't mind me telling you, she wanted to pack up douchebag's things. And since you've played white knight for her before, I should add I just saw Jeremy walk out the door and he didn't look happy."

He narrowed his gaze at the woman's surprising revelation. "Are you sure she'd want you telling me all this?"

"You? I'm positive. You can find her at…" She proceeded to ramble off Samantha's address. "In case you don't have it. Oh, and I'll have the doorman let you up. I have the code to add you to her list. Nice talking to you, Dex. Bye."

Brandy disconnected the call, leaving him with his phone in his hand and Samantha's address on repeat in his head.

THE LOCKSMITH WORKED on the front door while Samantha sat in the kitchen with her brother, relaying all the information she'd been keeping from him. By the time she finished, Ian had run his hand through his hair so many times, the strands stood on end.

"No prenup? Have I taught you nothing?" He rose

from his chair in her living room, pulled on his tie to loosen it, and began to pace. "Thank God you didn't marry the motherfucker or I'd have to have him killed."

"Ian!"

"What? Am I wrong?" Before she could do any more than shake her head, he held out his arms and she walked into them. He wrapped her in his brotherly warmth and kissed the top of her head.

"It's going to be okay. I texted you the best business lawyer in Manhattan. Call him as soon as you can." He released her and she stepped back, grateful for her big brother. No matter how nervous she'd been to tell him, he'd come through for her in the end.

"Okay I've got to get going but if you need me, don't hesitate to ask and I'll come back."

She smiled. "Give those kids a hug from Aunt Samantha, and thank you, Ian. Love you."

"I love you too." Turning, he left her apartment.

The locksmith finished his job a few minutes after Ian departed. Samantha paid him and closed the door, turning the deadbolt with a satisfied smile on her face.

She poured herself a glass of wine, because what was a good purging and cleansing without a celebratory drink and putting Taylor Swift on speaker? Then she began her mission: throwing Jeremy's things into large boxes she'd had delivered to the apartment before she left the office. Her ex was a neat freak, so she tossed his things in haphazardly, not bothering to fold the shirts and sweaters, all the while envisioning the aggravated expression on his face.

Her plan was to text and tell him to come get his things and if he gave her a hard time, she had no problem calling the police to have him evicted. After all, his name was not on the lease.

After an hour of work, she needed a break. The music still played about broken hearts and betrayal and she let herself mourn. Not for Jeremy, she knew getting rid of him was a gift she should have given herself a long time ago. But for the life she thought she wanted and would have. So she kept Taylor playing and lowered herself onto the sofa.

No sooner had she sat down than she heard sounds from the hallway outside the apartment and seconds later, banging on the door. Apparently she wouldn't have to text Jeremy to come here after all.

She braced herself for the confrontation to come, rose to her feet, walked to the door, and opened it. Jeremy stood on the other side, fist raised to knock again, his cheeks flushed red with anger.

"Jeremy! You saved me a call. Come on in. You can start dragging your boxes to the elevator. Or you can go downstairs for a luggage cart. Or, if you aren't feeling up to exerting the effort, I'm sure the doorman will help you. As long as you tip him, seeing as you aren't a tenant in this building."

"You can't do this, Samantha. I live here."

"Lived here. And only because I allowed it. Now I don't. So take your things and get out." She made a show of glancing at her watch. "You have ten minutes."

He shoved her aside, literally put his hands on her shoulders and pushed her out of his way, walking toward the bedroom.

Startled, she stared after him and drew a deep breath, trying to relax and breathe until he was gone. Jeremy was an arrogant, gaslighting jackass, but he'd never touched her in anger before.

Swallowing hard, she left the door open, feeling somewhat safer if someone could hear her, and walked to the windows overlooking the city. Jeremy's voice carried from inside the bedroom, though she couldn't make out the specifics of his conversation. A few minutes later, a knock sounded and she looked up to see Andrew, the doorman, standing with the luggage cart.

"Hi, Andrew."

"Hello, Ms. Dare. Mr. Rollins asked me to bring the cart up for him."

She smiled. "Thanks. You can leave it there. He'll be loading it up and heading down soon."

With a nod, he turned and strode down the hall, his footsteps sounding as he walked to the elevator.

Jeremy came out a few minutes later, dragging a box behind him. "I can't believe you rolled up one hundred percent cashmere," he muttered, picking up the box near the door.

"It's summer. You have plenty of time to get them dry cleaned." She leaned against the window and watched as he hefted the box onto the cart and stormed back inside.

"What did you say?" he asked, stalking toward her.

"I said you have plenty of time to get them cleaned," she said, enunciating each word.

He entered her personal space and she stiffened. With the window behind her, she felt trapped. He stood way too close, giving her a whiff of his over-powering cologne, which she'd never loved but now turned her stomach.

"Back up," she said, her tone firm.

"You've pushed me to my limit today." His voice rose and once again he was red in the face, his voice rising. "I agreed to let Marley go and now you're throwing me out of the place I've been living with no notice! Not to mention you disrespected my things—"

"You disrespected *me*, you cheating son of a bitch!"

He raised a hand and slapped her. Stunned, she

stared at him, her hand resting on her heated, hurting cheek.

Equally shocked, he gaped back. "Samantha, I didn't mean—"

Before she could catch her breath or process the pain, Jeremy went stumbling. She blinked away the tears and saw Dex holding her ex up by his shirt, arm pulled back, ready to throw a punch.

"Dex, no! He's not worth it. Please, just make him leave." Her cheek stung, she wanted an ice pack and time alone to breathe.

His hand shook as he turned toward her. Something he saw penetrated his fury because he released Jeremy who tripped and scrambled back.

Eyes narrowed, jaw clenched, he said, "Get the fuck out and don't bother her again."

Still pale, Jeremy looked from Samantha to Dex, who was more muscular and taller than him. "Send the rest of my things downstairs and I'll come get them," he said, and rushed out.

"Jesus, sweetheart." He stepped forward and placed a gentle hand under her chin, examining her cheek.

"How bad is it?" she asked, still stunned anyone would hit her.

"Just a light handprint," he said through gritted teeth.

She sensed from his rigid stance, he was holding back his anger while he took care of her and she was so grateful he'd shown up when he had.

"Come on. Let's get you some ice." He put his arm around her waist and led her to her kitchen. She directed him around the apartment and soon, he had an ice pack wrapped in a soft T-shirt and pressed it to her cheek. "Okay?" he asked.

"Yes. I can hold it." She gingerly took over. "What are you doing here?" she finally thought to ask.

He was leaning against the wood cabinets, his gaze on hers. "I've been worried about you. What you would be going through when you faced Jeremy again. Turns out I was right to be concerned."

She still felt the anger in him pulsing beneath the surface but to her, he was sweet and kind. "I'm glad you were here," she admitted.

Though Jeremy appeared stunned after he'd slapped her, she was aware enough to realize if he did it once, there was a good chance he'd do it again. She shivered at the prospect.

Dex stepped closer, *his* scent delicious and arousing. "I want to kill him for hurting you."

"Why do I find that sexy?" She ran her tongue over her bottom lip.

He reached for her chin again and rubbed his thumb over her jawline. "Once again, we have bad timing."

"I'm not drunk," she said, staring at her lips.

"No, you're hurt." He dipped his head and brushed his lips over hers. "Don't worry. There will be a right time. I intend to make sure of it."

Her entire body trembled with need but her cheek throbbed and she knew Dex had a point. How could she think about him when Jeremy and her messy life stood between them? On the other hand, how could she not?

# Chapter Ten

Dex helped Samantha settle. He stayed for dinner to make sure she ate something, but mostly so she wasn't alone. It also allowed time for him to calm down. If he'd walked out of the apartment in the spiraling state he'd been in, he'd have gone after Jeremy Rollins and that wouldn't have helped anyone, especially Samantha.

They sat side by side on the couch after agreeing on a *Fast & Furious* movie. But instead of watching, she lowered the volume. "I'm sorry, Dex. I've been nothing but trouble for you since the day we re-met."

She looked so vulnerable in the pale yellow pajama shorts and matching sweatshirt she wore. The hood wasn't over her head but the way it curled around her neck seemed to help cuddle her in its warmth. The desire to pull her into his arms and finish the job was strong, but as usual, it wasn't the time.

She had things on her mind, incorrect assumptions he needed to correct. "Who says you've been trouble?" He leaned in closer. "I've enjoyed almost hitting you with my car, saving you from the unwanted wedding, joining you in the Bahamas, and playing your knight in shining armor again today. I just wish I'd arrived sooner. Today, I mean." Reaching out, he wound a strand of her hair around his forefinger and rubbed his thumb over the soft piece.

"I think you were just in time." Her palm went to her cheek and she sighed. "He's never raised a hand to me before. Nobody's ever hit me before." She tucked her legs against her chest and wrapped her arms around them.

"Nobody should hit you *ever*." Dex flexed his fingers and reminded himself she didn't need his anger. "I think you should call a lawyer. See if you can get a restraining order to keep that bastard away from you."

"Ian gave me the name of a corporate attorney to discuss breaking up the partnership."

"Good. And I'm sure he has a partner who does domestic law. Why don't you give him a call in the morning?"

She nodded. "I will. Now, can we stop talking about Jeremy?"

"Sure. Want to watch the movie?" He gestured to the television. "I can start it over."

She smiled at the offer. "I've seen it, but thanks. Can I ask you some questions, instead?"

He didn't know what she had in mind but if it soothed her nerves, he was all for it. "Sure. Shoot."

She slid her feet down until they hit the floor and

turned toward him. "If you don't want to talk about these things, it's fine. And I know I'm being nosey, but I'm curious."

Now she had *him* curious.

"You told me you were adopted. What made you take the Sterling last name instead of keeping your own? What *was* your last name, anyway?" She waved her hand through the air. "Again, you don't have to tell me, I just—"

"Initially, I didn't become a Sterling. I agreed to the adoption and was happy to be part of the family. Nobody treated me like I wasn't a real sibling. Even our grandparents took me into the fold."

She clasped her hands over her chest. "I love that for you."

"I did too. Then I grew up and I started having these recurring dreams. Except they were grounded in reality. My biological parents fought. A lot."

"About what?" She scooted in closer to him, making it easier for him to answer.

"Anything. Everything. They didn't need a reason. Which was why I spent so much time next door, with Remy's family. His parents didn't argue much and they were normal and loving. Until Mom was killed… but I really don't want to talk about that tonight."

There was only so much he could reveal at one time. Especially about a past he rarely talked about and had never told a woman in his life.

"Okay," she said softly. "We can change the subject."

"I'll tell you about my parents. I want to." He wouldn't mind getting the words out and maybe cut into the occasional nightmare that still plagued him.

She moved closer and took his hand. "I'm listening." She held on and didn't let go.

"The fights were ugly. It never turned physical but it was always bad. The best I could hope for was that they held their anger until they were home but there were many times the other parents on the bleachers got a show."

She winced. "I'm so sorry. I thought praying my dad would make it to events and having him always be a no-show was bad."

He clocked that bit of information to discuss with her another time. As much as she wanted to know him, he had the same desire to dig deeper into what and who had created Samantha. The woman who intrigued him on a deeper level than any had before.

"There's no point in comparing sucky childhoods. We both had our own trauma."

"Okay, so go on."

She still held his hand and he didn't want her to let go. "The night they died, I had a babysitter over. A college girl who often watched me when they went out. It felt late when the police knocked on the door. I'm sure you can imagine the rest."

"Oh, Dex. I'm so sorry. Is that the dream? About finding out?"

He shook his head. "The dream is what I overheard one of the officers tell Alex, my dad now. A witness saw my mother reach for the steering wheel before my father lost control. In other words, they were having one of their arguments." His voice sounded hoarse as he explained. "I—"

"Dex," she said, cutting him off. "I didn't think asking about your last name would lead to you reliving a nightmare. I'm sorry. You don't have to continue." She squeezed his hand tighter and he was grateful for her empathy.

"It's fine. I suddenly feel the need to share this with you."

"Okay," she whispered. "I'm here." She cuddled in closer and when he breathed in, her warm, familiar scent eased his tension.

He covered her hand with his free one. "The fight, at least in the dream, is about me. I just hear my father yell my name, my mother screams something back and grabs for the wheel. Then the sound of grating, crashing metal… And I wake up." In a sweat, shaking. The way he felt now, revealing the rawest part of himself.

She rose to her knees and wrapped her arms around his neck. "Dex, I'm so sorry. That's a burden no child should have to live with. I'm not surprised it haunts you as an adult."

"It doesn't happen often anymore." He embraced her, drawing comfort that quickly turned to something more. The heat of her body pressed against his and the warmth of her breath against his cheek was more than he could take after thinking of her nonstop since leaving the Bahamas.

She lifted her head and met his gaze. Her lips parted. And he waited, giving her time to pull back. But Samantha knew her mind. She placed her palms against his cheeks, leaned in, and pressed her lips to his.

Fireworks exploded between them and Dex took control, shifting positions so he could ease her down onto the sofa, his body hovering over hers.

He kissed her thoroughly, his tongue delving into her mouth, then trailing his lips over her jawbone and continuing down her neck, nipping at her lightly before reaching the barrier of her heavy sweatshirt collar. She reached for the hem and pulled the bulky garment over her head, leaving her exposed. And braless. Damn. Good thing he hadn't known she'd been bare beneath it.

Her dusky nipples had hardened into tight peaks

and the desire to taste her was strong. After waiting so long, knowing he had free rein over her body was heady. He slid his hands up her silky skin, along her sides, and pulled a nipple into his mouth, tasting and tormenting it with his tongue and teeth.

Cupping the other breast in his hand, he gave it equal attention and she moaned her approval, wrapping her legs around his. Their bodies ground together, pleasure and pain a mix because holding back wasn't easy. His cock was hard, the need to feel her pulse around his dick strong so he pushed himself off her and rose to his feet.

He stripped off his clothes in a rush. Once naked, he turned to focus on Samantha, assuming she'd done the same. She still had her bottoms on but her eyes were dark and dilated, her stare focused on him.

"See something you like, sweetheart?" He raked his gaze over her bare breasts. "Because I know I do."

She ran her tongue over her damp bottom lip and his dick pulsed in response.

"I take it our timing is better now?" she asked.

"You tell me." Unable to help himself, he gripped his hard length and gave it a firm tug.

"It's perfect," she said in a husky voice, as she hooked her thumbs into the waistband of her shorts and maneuvered them down, revealing her pussy with a narrow landing strip.

He swallowed hard. "It sure is." He needed to taste her glistening sex and he needed to do it now.

He scooped her into his arms and walked straight to her bedroom, depositing her on the bed. He grasped her thighs and pulled her to the edge, then slammed his hands down on either side of her hips. Dipping his head, he slid his tongue through her wet folds. Her hips arched and he held her down, palm on her stomach, and proceeded to devour her, sucking, licking and teasing until she writhed beneath him.

He spent a good five minutes bringing her to the brink of orgasm, feeling the little spasms as she got close and the flutters around his tongue. She'd moan loudly and he'd pull away, only to dive in to tease her again.

She threaded her fingers through his hair and as his tongue moved away from her clit, she clutched his strands and yanked hard. "Dex, please!"

He lifted his head. She'd done the same and he met her frantic gaze. "Please what?" he asked, taking in her flushed cheeks.

"Make me come, Dex. Please, I need to come."

The words were all he needed. He slid one finger into her warm heat and dipped his head to finish what he'd started. All it took was consecutive pumps of his finger, then curling it against the right spot, joined by one swipe of his tongue, and she came apart.

Her body shook and she cried out his name as her climax crashed over her. He eased her down, drawing out every last shudder, then wiped his mouth on her thigh and met her hazy gaze.

"Tell me you have protection," he said. He hadn't been with a woman in a while and he didn't make it a habit of carrying a condom in his wallet.

"Thank God there are some in the nightstand over there." She gestured behind her.

Neither said it but he could see the relief in her gaze as she probably realized she'd used the right kind of birth control with a cheating asshole ex. Not someone he wanted to think about now or he'd lose his erection.

After grabbing a foil from the drawer, he ripped it open and rolled it over his cock before walking back around the bed. She hadn't moved from where he'd left her. Her legs were bent, feet against the edge of the mattress. Prime position for what he had in mind.

"Ready, sweetheart?"

"I've been waiting, Dex. What took you so long?" A naughty gleam flickered in her eyes.

"Brat," he said with a grin, lifting first one leg and placing it over his shoulder, then doing the same with the other before lifting her ass so she was level with his dick.

One thrust and he entered her, his eyes nearly rolling back in his head at how perfect she felt, hot and wet around his cock. If he'd known how right they fit way back when, he would never have been able to stay away.

SAMANTHA'S NERVES TINGLED with awareness, her body still coming down from her last orgasm as Dex entered her, their bodies joining with a smooth thrust. He was thick and long and she felt him everywhere, in the best possible ways.

Before she could do more than process his size, he pulled back and pushed deep. With her legs over his shoulders and him holding her tight, she had no control over her orgasm, but it didn't matter because Dex knew what he was doing. How to angle himself to hit just the right spot, when to shift back and press forward again.

She was used to missionary, quick movements, and it was over, at least for Jeremy, leaving her empty. With Dex, she felt full and everything he did brought her higher, her need to climax again building.

"Come for me, sweetheart, because I'm close."

Another difference. He waited for her. Slowed down, making her body aware of the difference, and it worked, every nerve ending responding to his whims as he lit her up inside. Suddenly she tipped over the cliff, waves of warmth and utter perfection washing over her.

"Oh God, Dex. I'm coming."

With those words, he let himself go, taking over her body, pushing in, pulling out, each movement faster and with more intensity. He stopped holding back and took her hard.

"Yes," she said. "More."

He responded, those gorgeous blue eyes staring into hers until he stilled with a groan, his climax triggering another one of her own.

A few seconds later, he helped her bend her legs and move them onto the floor, dangling off the bed. "Be right back."

He disappeared into her bathroom and she managed to scoot back on the bed, flopping against the pillows, sated and relaxed.

To her surprise, he returned with a towel and helped her clean up. "You're the perfect gentleman," she murmured. No point in thinking of her past when the present was so amazing.

Once he'd settled in bed, she took her turn in the bathroom, glancing in the mirror. Her cheeks were flushed, her eyes dilated, and her hair a mess. Only one thing marred the just-been-fucked-in-the-best-way look. The handprint had faded but a red patch remained.

She still couldn't believe Jeremy had hit her. Thank God Dex had shown up when he had. Later, when the orgasmic haze wore off, she'd think of all the reasons this had been a bad idea, but right now she pushed all heavy thoughts away. She deserved this one night of bliss with the shambles of a life that was waiting for her tomorrow.

She walked out of the bathroom. Dex sat against the headboard, bare-chested with one arm behind his head, looking sexier than ever.

She sat down on the mattress. He immediately pulled her into his arms and she curled around him, resting her head on his shoulder and inhaling his delicious scent. Something about him calmed her.

"That was spectacular," he said, his voice a low grumble.

She couldn't contain the pleased smile that came to her lips. "It really was."

"Thanks again for showing up when I needed you." She didn't think she could say that enough.

"No thanks necessary. I'm relieved I was there. But I'm beginning to think I have a sixth sense when it comes to rescuing you, Ms. Dare."

His finger twisted around a long strand of her hair and she sighed. "I'm grateful but I definitely need to stand up for myself when needed."

"I know you can handle yourself but give that lawyer a call and see what your options are."

She nodded. "Creating a hostile work environment for myself and my employees may not be it."

She believed Jeremy's slap had startled him enough to prevent it from happening again. Especially at work, but she intended to make sure she was never alone with him.

"Enough talk about your ex," he said, rolling her onto her back and coming over her, his erection thick against her sex.

"Again?" she asked, surprised.

"Any objections?"

She stared into his gorgeous face and shook her head. "Not one."

His lips came down on hers and she forgot everything except Dex.

# Chapter Eleven

A FEW DAYS later, Dex met with his old teammate Wes at The Back Door. He decided to ask Remy to sit in, to see if his brother was interested in the clothing business idea. Wes had a sister, Ines, who'd gone viral on social media with her designs and together, the four of them had agreed to make the concept a reality. Lawyers would have to get involved but for today, they had a handshake start to the deal.

After Wes and Ines left, Dex joined Remy in his office so they could talk. Each sat in the chairs across from the desk, side by side.

His brother turned his way. "What's got you in such a good mood?" Remy asked. "If I didn't know better, I'd say you'd just gotten laid."

Dex cocked an eyebrow. "What the fuck does that mean? I can get a woman if I wanted to."

Remy smirked. "No kidding but for the last I don't know how long, nobody's interested you."

"Maybe I've just gotten more selective in my old age."

Considering they both recently turned thirty-one, Remy burst out laughing. "Okay, since you aren't going to offer up information, I'll just ask. Is Samantha the reason for that perpetual grin on your face?"

Dex took a long sip of his beer, deciding whether or not he wanted to get into his personal life here and now. Before he could reply, his cell rang.

A glance told him it was a FaceTime call and the caller was Ian Dare. "Aah, shit. I have to take this."

"I'll go find my wife and catch up with you before you leave." Remy pushed back his chair and rose to his feet.

Once alone, he swiped his phone. "Ian. To what do I owe the pleasure?" Dex asked.

Ian's face showed on the screen. He'd obviously returned home to Miami and was at work, as Dex recognized the renovated stadium photo on the wall behind the man's desk.

"I just hung up with my sister."

Which could mean he wanted to speak about any number of things. "And?" Dex didn't typically play coy but no point in showing his hand before he had to.

He had no idea what, if anything, Samantha would tell her brother about them. Nor did he know where *they* stood. He'd said goodbye to her with a long kiss the morning after, leaving her in bed so he could head home, change, and work out before his first meeting of the day.

"That son of a bitch hit her."

Aah. This call made sense.

"I took care of it," Dex said. The only reason Jeremy Rollins wasn't ten feet under was because Samantha had begged him to let the man just leave. Okay, that was an exaggeration, but at the very least Dex would have liked to hit him hard enough to break his jaw. That would have given him a sense of satisfaction.

"She told me, and I appreciate you being there for her."

Dex decided it was time for a long overdue talk. "Aren't you going to ask me *why* I was at your sister's?"

"I assume you'd tell me what Samantha did. That it's none of my business," Ian said.

"Yet you made it your business at the Thunder's New Year's Eve party."

Dex drummed his fingers on the edge of his brother's desk. No matter where this conversation went, he was all in with Samantha. Knowing her current situation, he didn't expect her to feel the same but that didn't mean he wouldn't be there for her while she pulled the pieces of her life back together.

"She was just a kid, then."

"Over twenty-one, but you made your point and I was just starting out. I wasn't going to fuck up my career with the Thunder. But I'm not afraid of blow-back anymore."

Ian chuckled, the bastard. "Well, you have my approval anyway. Samantha can do worse than someone who protects her when her family can't be there."

Dex rolled his eyes at the arrogance of the man. But he'd feel the same in Fallon's case. Still, Ian didn't need to know that.

"I don't need your approval anymore, Ian." But he'd be lying if he didn't feel better knowing he had it. Samantha idolized her brother and she was going through enough. She didn't need Dex complicating things further.

"And that's why you have it anyway. Good talking to you, Dex. Oh, and another thing. The lawyer said a slap isn't enough to get a restraining order without having Jeremy arrested and charged with domestic violence or assault. And Samantha feels it's too late. So I assume you'll be making your presence known in my sister's life so that bastard knows what fear feels like."

Samantha wouldn't like Dex playing bodyguard but if he did it in a smooth enough way, she'd see interest not meddling. It meant a lot to her to stand on her own two feet. He'd just be there to support her because Jeremy wasn't laying a hand on her again.

"Ian?"

"Hmm?"

"Go back to work and let me live my life. I've got your sister's back."

Ian disconnected the call without saying goodbye.

SAMANTHA SAT AT her desk, unable to concentrate on a new client. Given how important the account was to the firm and how distracted Samantha was, she decided to hand off the work to her top VP. She even cut herself slack as she made the decision because there was no doubt Samantha was in a transitional time of her life.

The apartment she'd tossed Jeremy out of might be hers but it had too many memories of a man she now despised. There was no doubt that having Dex in her bed had helped stamp out unwanted reminders but the uncomfortable feeling when she was there remained. She wasn't up to moving right now but the idea was floating in the back of her mind.

It helped that she'd managed not to see Jeremy for the first three days after Dex Day, as she'd come to call their night together. Better than calling it the day Jeremy had slapped her and being forced to think about it all the time.

She was still furious with her ex but thanks to Ian's connections, she'd already met with Tim Daley, the business attorney he'd recommended. The wheels were in motion to request a buyout of Jeremy's portion of the firm. As the attorney explained, these things normally moved slowly but he understood the urgency in her situation.

Tim had called in one of his partners, a criminal attorney who'd doled out bad news. Despite the slap, there was nothing she could do to keep Jeremy out of the office and away from her. He cited lack of evidence. She hadn't taken photos of her red face, nor had she reported the incident to the police. The one act without proof or an arrest for domestic assault would not be enough for a restraining order, temporary or not, especially one that would impact a place of business.

On the positive side, Ian was a huge client of Tim's and he handled most of the team's legal affairs, so he was willing to rush the push for a buyout, if Jeremy would even consider it. Given how much he liked money, Samantha held on to hope.

For now, she had to steer clear of her ex, which hadn't been difficult given the distance between their two offices. The day after his shocking behavior, he'd met her at the elevator with flowers and apologies. She'd told him to shove the *I'm sorry*s and tossed the flowers in the trash. He'd left her alone ever since.

Dex hadn't. To her surprise, he'd shown up daily,

the times varying. The first morning, he arrived with a latte, guessing what she preferred and getting it wrong. But he'd introduced her to a new favorite flavor. Caramel. The next day, he showed up with flowers, stopping by on his way to a meeting. These blooms she kept on her desk in her direct line of vision, liking the reminder that Dex cared.

He was quickly becoming part of her life and whenever she was alone, her thoughts would drift to him and their time together, and not just the one incredible night of mind-blowing sex. The long talks they'd shared both in the Bahamas and in New York had gone deep, and she'd revealed more to him than she'd ever done with Jeremy.

Dex's playful banter during intimacy was new and refreshing. His protective nature merely added to his appeal. And the sex? She squirmed at the thought of her legs over his shoulders, him focused on making sure she came first.

Dex Sterling was a special man. But her life was a cluster and every self-help book she'd skimmed said not to jump into another romance too fast. But did that mean she couldn't have Dex in her life? Friends with benefits suited her just fine and based on his past, Dex didn't seem to be in the market for a serious relationship either.

And she wasn't ready to give him up.

A knock sounded on her door. Knowing Brandy was outside and would let her know if she was leaving her desk, she called, "Come in!" without worrying about Jeremy being on the other side.

Dex strode into the room, a bag of food with the name of a restaurant she recognized in hand.

She rose from her chair, taking in his relaxed stance and clothing. Wearing a pair of black sweats and a gray T-shirt, those strong arms with flexing muscles called to her.

"Hi!" she said, happy to see him.

"Hey, beautiful."

At the endearment, her body warmed and she flushed under his heated gaze. "I hope you brought enough for two?" she asked.

"I wish I could stay and eat with you, but my sister asked me if I could help her move a few things around her gallery and I couldn't say no."

She smiled at that. "I'm sure she appreciates you."

"She does. You'd like Fallon," he said as he walked toward her desk and around to where she sat.

He sat on the desk and leaned close. "Tell me you're okay. That you feel safe here. Jeremy's leaving you alone?"

She nodded. "I honestly think he scared himself. He wouldn't want to ruin his reputation at work any more than his affair with Marley has." She shuddered at the reminder.

"And she's gone?"

"From the office, yes. From his life? I don't know nor do I care," she said.

It was still hard to believe her anger outweighed the hurt. Even harder to wrap her head around the relief she actually felt that his cheating had saved her from marrying him. She'd been stuffing down so much unhappiness she was just letting bubble to the surface now. Every day she processed something new about her old life. When she wasn't thinking of Dex, that is.

"Where did you go?" he asked.

"Sorry. I was just musing about how I'm so much more angry than hurt." She raised her shoulders in a small shrug. "And then I was thinking about you."

He leaned in, closing the distance between them, and pressed his lips to the sensitive spot behind her ear and she let out a low moan.

"I hear that sound in my sleep," he said in a gruff voice.

His rumbling voice caused her nipples to harden and peak behind her silk blouse, and her panties were now wet. She wasn't leaving this office anytime soon, she thought, doing her best not to cross her arms over her chest. She was so turned on, she couldn't come up with a coherent reply.

"I can't stop thinking of our night together." He kissed her jaw, then brushed his lips over hers. "And I can't stop thinking about you. Is a repeat on the agenda? After I take you to dinner?"

Her heart thumped hard in her chest at his suggestion. "On one condition." She'd been thinking about being with him again but she'd also considered what she needed in order to agree. To keep herself sane and not fall under another man's spell.

"Name it." The words were an order.

He didn't step away and his scent wrapped around her like a sexy blanket and her thoughts scattered. "Oh umm…"

"Breathe, beautiful." He ran a knuckle over her cheek. "And tell me what you need."

She flushed at how easily he distracted her. Which was the main reason for her setting ground rules. "I need you to know that I'm in a transitional stage of my life," she said, repeating what she'd been trying to convince herself of since he'd walked out of her apartment and she'd wanted to call him back for more.

"Understood."

She couldn't read much beyond his somber expression and tone.

"Which means this can't be anything serious."

He raised an eyebrow, cupped her face in his hands, and kissed her long and hard. He didn't come up for air, instead he breathed her in, his tongue twining with hers. She melted for him, giving whatever he asked for and more.

Nipping her bottom lip, he lifted his head. "Keep telling yourself that. I'll be away for the week on business, so promise if you have any trouble with Jeremy, this time you'll call the police."

She nodded. "I promise. Where are you going?"

"San Francisco to shoot some promotional commercials for the network."

She smiled. "Oooh, sounds fun." She'd miss him, not that she wanted to admit as much.

"About as fun as a torn rotator cuff, but it's part of the job." He frowned at the prospect, which made her feel better about him having to leave.

"I'll be back next Thursday. So I'll pick you up Friday night at your apartment." After another brief swipe of his lips, he stood and walked out the door, leaving her staring after his tight butt in those black sweats. It was a good thing nobody was here to see her drool.

# Chapter Twelve

DEX SPENT A long week in California doing his least favorite part of the broadcasting job. It was the reason he tried not to take advertising gigs like Brady and the Manning brothers did. Not to mention, this was the worst time for him to be away from the city and Samantha. He worried that Jeremy would show up when she was alone and defenseless, but he needed to trust her to be smart and not get caught alone with her ex.

His plans for the evening were set, thanks to having the right connections and people willing to do favors. But first he had a meeting with his agent and headed to the Meridian NYC to meet up with Austin Prescott. Though Austin lived in Miami, he was in town to see clients and he'd requested an early lunch meeting.

He gave his car to the valet at the hotel where he'd met up with Samantha over two weeks ago. It was hard to believe how much his life and outlook had changed in that short span of time. When he'd pulled into the circular drive the first time, his focus had been his career. Now he caught himself thinking about

Samantha as part of whatever his plans were for the future.

Once he was in the restaurant, he caught sight of Austin sitting with his personal assistant and wife, Quinn. She'd been Austin's right hand for over a year before one of his ex's left a baby girl on his doorstep and he'd called Quinn for help. Next thing anyone knew, Austin and Quinn were a solid couple and neither had looked back.

He strode over to the table and stopped by Quinn. "I'm glad you're here too," he said, leaning over to kiss her cheek before turning to his agent. "Austin." They shook hands and Dex joined them at the table.

"How's Jenny?" he asked.

"Five going on twenty," Austin said with a shake of his head.

Quinn chuckled. "But she's a daddy's girl," she said with a smile. And of course, she pulled out her phone and showed him a picture of the little cutie in high ponytails on either side of her head.

"She's adorable," he said with a chuckle.

"And a handful. But Austin's mom agreed to watch her while we came to New York on business."

Austin reached over and took his wife's hand and placed a kiss on top. "Not just business," he said in a gruff voice.

"Okay, we might go way back but I don't need to

hear that." Dex gestured for the server and ordered an Arnold Palmer.

"Refills?" he asked the couple.

After they answered, Austin straightened in his seat. "So… business," he said, his lips pulled in a tight line. "Ian mentioned you helped out his sister."

Great. The Dare family gossip tree was going strong. Austin was a Dare by blood. Paul Dare, Samantha's uncle, was the Prescott kids' sperm donor dad. The only reason Dex knew the details was because he and Austin had become friends over the years Austin had represented him.

Dex glared at his agent, not thrilled with his personal life being up for discussion. "I was there for her," he said, deliberately being vague.

"By taking her to the Bahamas?" Austin asked, his voice low and his tone grim.

Dex curled his hands into fists on his lap. "Austin, you're my agent and a friend, but I have to ask, why the hell is this your business?"

Quinn sat in silence, uncomfortable if the squirming in her seat was any indication.

"Optics." Bracing his arms on the table, Austin leaned forward, moving in closer for a quiet but firm conversation. "How do you think it looks if the network gets wind of the fact that you took a woman to a private home in the Bahamas on the same day she walked out on her wedding?"

Dex swallowed his anger. "After discovering the groom was not only cheating on her but planning to divorce her and take half her money? I think the sympathy vote comes down on Samantha's side."

"Look, she's my cousin and I feel sorry for her but the fact is, you signed with a family network. They aren't going to want you to be the subject of a scandal and they certainly won't want any distraction from football so close to when their new multimillion-dollar anchor is set to go on the air."

"This is all bullshit," Dex muttered. "What are you asking me to do, Austin? Stay away from her? Because that's not going to happen." Frustration boiled in his gut at the thought. "And I expect my agent to have my back." His voice rose as the ramifications of this conversation became clear.

"I do have your back but part of my job is telling you the truth. You have a morality clause in your contract and a lot on the line." Austin's decibel level matched Dex's.

"Austin, we don't need to give the press a story here, either." Quinn put a hand on her husband's arm. The gesture got his attention and his entire body relaxed.

She might have diffused her husband's anger but Dex was still furious. "My personal life is just that.

Samantha is no longer engaged and she never married, so she's free to see whoever she wants. Tell the network that if they come to you with any complaints."

Austin let out a slow breath and nodded. "I understand your perspective. I was just looking out for your best interest. I do think it would be best if you and Samantha kept things quiet until more time has passed. Going public so soon could have blowback. As your agent, that's all I'm saying. As your friend and her cousin, I just want you both to be happy."

Dex nodded, his anger leaving as quickly as it had come. "Samantha's been through a lot lately. She doesn't deserve the shit Jeremy put her through and I won't make her feel like I'm hiding her. That said, we haven't defined our relationship, so it's premature to jump to any conclusions."

"Understood."

"I'd also appreciate it if you didn't mention this conversation or your opinion on the matter to Samantha." Dex didn't need her backing away in some misguided attempt to protect him. She had enough reasons to be wary of relationships without adding Austin's paranoia to the mix.

Austin narrowed his gaze. "Really? I think you'd trust my professionalism by now."

Quinn let out a deep sigh. "Everyone's made their

point. I suggest we move on to food now," she said in a tone that didn't allow for argument.

Austin placed his hand over hers and Dex respected her enough to listen, too. The rest of the meeting consisted of catching up on a friendlier level and talk about the media coaching he'd done with a professional Austin had put him in contact with while in California. Between Dex's knowledge of the sport and already being comfortable in front of the camera for all the post-game press conferences, he was ready for the job.

"What about your house on Star Island? Are you planning to sell?" Austin asked.

Dex rubbed the back of his neck. "Unsure. I do have clothing and some things there I want to go back for, but part of me wants to hang on to the property."

"A vacation home?" Quinn asked.

"Maybe." He could see bringing Samantha there to share what the place meant to him.

When he'd signed his first million-dollar contract, the idea of owning a huge house had been appealing, but he found his penthouse more comfortable and homey than an overly large mansion. Still, the home represented something apart from the money he'd inherited and he was proud of it.

They discussed various football teams' potential for the year and soon, the brunch was almost over.

When Austin asked what his plans were for the weekend, Dex hedged, not revealing the date he had in store for Samantha.

It was nobody's business but theirs.

SAMANTHA SLIPPED INTO her favorite sundress, a yellow-and-white floral that hit above the knee. She was just hooking her strappy sandals when a ding on her phone alerted her that she had company coming up, and her stomach fluttered with anticipation. Though she'd heard from Dex while he was away, she'd spent the week in a heightened state of anxiety at work.

Where Jeremy was concerned, what her lawyers considered moving fast and what she'd hoped for were two separate things. She kept expecting him to walk into her office, angry and out of control. At least tonight's date with Dex had given her something pleasurable to look forward to. More so since just hearing his deep voice on the phone made her girly parts extremely happy, which had led to her giving her vibrator a workout.

She glanced in the bedroom mirror, took a quick look at the light coating of makeup she'd put on, and wondered if Dex preferred to kiss glossed or matte lips. She shrugged and reapplied her lipstick, pressed her lips together, and was ready to go.

She grabbed her purse and walked to the entry just as a knock sounded and she opened the door to let Dex in. He stood before her in a pair of dark jeans and a light blue collared button-up shirt that set off his sexy eyes. He'd rolled the sleeves, revealing those muscles she loved to ogle.

Her gaze slid to his to find him devouring her the same way she'd been doing to him. He let out a low whistle. "I think we have to upgrade you from beautiful to gorgeous." Stepping forward, he clasped his hands around her waist and leaned in for a light kiss on her cheek.

She breathed in his scent. Her body tingled, and she wished he'd kiss her on the lips.

Instead, he stepped back. "Come on. We're on a schedule."

"Where are we going?" she asked, as he slipped his hand in hers.

"It's a surprise, remember?" He waited as she locked up, set the alarm, and they took off.

He'd driven his Mercedes and they ended up in Midtown where he parked in a lot and gave the Benz to a valet, sliding money into the man's hand to take care of the vehicle.

He clasped their fingers together and led her down

the sidewalk, the warm summer air wafting around them. "I hope you like pizza."

"Love it." Her stomach rumbled in agreement.

He led her to a typical New York City pizza place that was ultra-casual. They ordered a large pizza at the counter, then sat down to wait until Dex could walk back and pick up their food.

They talked about his photo shoot in San Francisco and how much he despised being in front of the camera like a model but was looking forward to live broadcasts of the games and discussing the plays as they happened.

A man behind the counter called out their order and Dex stood, walking over to collect their pizza and two sodas. Once he settled into his seat across from her, he handed her a slice and she took a bite, chewing and savoring the piece.

"You cannot get pizza like this in Florida," she said. "It's one of the perks of living in the city."

"This is my favorite pizza spot and I'm happy to share it with you."

She took another bite and moaned. "I hope they deliver uptown."

"Do not make that sound in public where I can't react to it the way I want to."

A glance at him showed his cheeks were flushed and his gaze darkened.

"Oops." She grinned but also squirmed because she felt the same desire oozing through her veins.

He shook his head and after he ate some, he said, "Back to your point, they have another restaurant close to where you live that I'm sure will deliver."

"Excellent." She was already planning in her mind.

"So, you're good with being here? Really?" He gestured around the place that had filled up with couples, families, and kids. "As opposed to someplace fancy, I mean."

She leaned forward. "Dex, I realize you don't know me well yet, so let me enlighten you. I don't need expensive meals or restaurants. I just like spending time with you. What kind of women have you been dating, anyway?"

Interesting question, he thought. "Well, I can't say I've been dating much but during my career, women were all about what I could buy for them, where I could take them, and who they could meet when they were with me. I found it hard to make a real connection and given that I was so football focused, I never really tried."

She hated thinking about him floundering as women tried to use him for his money and fame. "That's sad. I can promise you my mom raised us right. We all appreciate things being real." Everything her mom hadn't had with her father.

He narrowed his gaze. "You seem sad. Does valuing people and not things have anything to do with your father's betrayal?" he asked.

She nodded, aware that he was ultra-sensitive to her moods and thoughts. Something else that was new to her in a relationship. Not that they were in one. Or were they?

"My father was good at buying us off," she admitted. "He'd come home from *business trips*," she said, using finger quotes, "with gifts for the kids and expensive jewelry for Mom. When we were younger it was exciting. As we grew up, we understood we'd rather have our father at school events than presents and a quick visit. And when we found out he wasn't working but was raising another family, every illusion we had shattered."

He reached over, putting his big, warm hand over hers. "I'm sorry. That's horrible. But you keep saying when *we* found out, *we* understood… but how did *you* feel?"

She swallowed hard. "There were so many of us, we've always been a *we*. The Dare kids." She nibbled on her bottom lip. "I guess it's just easier to lump us together than to deal with my personal feelings about my father."

As if sensing there was more, Dex waited patiently. The noise around them faded until it was just the two of them and she could think.

"My feelings never mattered," she said honestly. "I was worried about my siblings. I saw them being strong, so I emulated them. I thought if I fell apart then they'd have to worry about me too. Especially Ian. He took on everyone's pain."

Dex's hand squeezed tighter. "You matter, Samantha. Your feelings, your pain, it's yours and it's okay to own it."

He hesitated and she processed his words, a lump growing larger in her throat the longer he was silent.

"Is that why you haven't really broken down about Jeremy?" he asked. "Because you're so used to stuffing your feelings down deep?"

She shook her head. "I haven't broken down because I didn't love him, but you're right. I also haven't allowed myself to feel real hurt over losing the life I wanted—not the man but the future I'd hoped for. The career, a husband, kids. I wanted what my mom never got. I wanted my kids to have what my dad never gave me. And I fucked up and chose the wrong man." She wrapped her goosebump covered arms around herself.

Dex was out of his seat and sliding into her side of the booth in an instant. He wrapped an arm around her shoulders and pulled her close.

"Just because you chose wrong once doesn't mean

you'll never see your dreams come true." He kissed her temple. "Once you get through the rubble, you'll see a whole new future ahead of you. As long as you remember that what *you* want matters."

She leaned into him and sighed. "You're a good guy, Dex. Solid. Thanks for this talk."

"I didn't mean for things to get so heavy but—"

"It's okay. I needed to face those emotions. So tell me," she said, eager to change the subject. "What's next on our agenda tonight? You said we're on a schedule."

"We are. I also said it's a surprise."

She rolled her eyes. "You're frustrating."

He let out a laugh. "And you're impatient. Are you finished eating?" he asked.

She nodded. "Yep."

"Then let's head to the main destination."

She was relieved to put the emotional drama away for the night and gathered their paper plates to toss in the garbage.

He slid out of the booth, then stood and held out a hand for her to do the same. After dumping the trash, they exited the pizza parlor and took a long walk, weaving through the crowds and ending up at a building she recognized.

"The Rooftop Cinema?" she asked, her excitement growing. "I read about this place but I haven't had the chance to check it out. Do we have good seats?"

His grin held a hint of mischief. "The best. Let's go see."

A few minutes later, he'd checked in with someone and she discovered Dex had rented out the entire third floor rooftop for them alone. All the chairs she'd seen in pictures online had been packed away and just two remained facing the large screen.

The man who'd escorted them up whispered something to Dex before he walked away, disappearing through the door leading inside.

"What did he say?"

"That the popcorn's over in the corner along with water bottles, soda, and blankets. Oh, and nobody will bother us or come in until the movie ends."

# Chapter Thirteen

AFTER DEX LEFT the earlier meeting with Austin and Quinn, he'd headed home, changed, and gone to the gym. He needed to slake his anger at Austin before he could process what his agent had been trying to say. As he'd bench-pressed weights, he didn't make conversation with the trainer spotting him. He just gave serious consideration to what Austin told him, ultimately accepting that the man was just doing his job.

Austin's words, along with Samantha's need to take things slow, led him to decide that he could live his life and be with her, as long as he was discreet. Taking Samantha for pizza was the equivalent of friends going for a meal and the movie was completely private.

He hadn't expected to get such insight into who Samantha was over pizza but he'd gotten it anyway. It was clear she needed someone who both saw and heard her, who recognized her needs in a way no one had before. And he wanted to be the man who gave that to her.

"This is amazing," she said, drawing his attention

back to the setting he'd planned. "You did this for us?"

"I wanted to give you something special."

She reached up on her toes, wrapped her arms around his neck, and hugged him, her happiness and gratitude obvious. But within an instant the rubbing of their bodies changed the gesture into more.

"Dex," she murmured, threading her fingers through his hair and scratching his scalp lightly with her nails.

God, he wanted to lay her out beneath the dark sky and devour her sweet body. "We have a movie to watch." He barely recognized his own desire-laden voice.

"I know. I wouldn't want your effort to go to waste."

He didn't give a damn about wasted effort, but he did want this experience with her. "Seats or blankets on the floor?" he asked.

She wrinkled her nose as she attempted to decide. "Blankets. I want to be close to you," she murmured.

That sounded good to him.

Together they gathered two blankets, setting them in front of the chairs, creating a comfortable space. Once they were seated, the movie began, a romantic comedy he'd chosen for her, telling himself he'd get through it. He'd watched enough when he'd taken

Fallon to the movies when they were younger.

But this was nothing like being with his sister. He settled Samantha between his legs as he leaned against the chair behind him. She leaned back into him and they watched the movie. To his surprise, it was fun and he tried to relax and ignore his hard-on, which he managed… until the love scene on the screen. It was graphic and Samantha squirmed in his arms, her arousal obvious.

He slid a hand up her dress and cupped one breast in his hand, pleased to find no bra. The movie continued on the screen but he was neither watching nor listening. He tweaked her nipple, rubbing it between his thumb and forefinger, not letting up or giving her relief. She moaned and twisted, trying to turn and face him, but that wasn't his plan. He continued to tweak and play with the tight bud until she was panting with need.

"Shh," he said into her ear. "I've got you."

She lay her head back against his shoulder. "I'm so empty, Dex. I need—"

"Tell me what you need, beautiful."

She pressed her palm against her obviously needy sex and he pulled her hand away. "No. If you're going to come, it will be because I'm letting you."

His cock throbbed against the confining material of his pants but his needs would have to wait.

He replaced her hand with his, letting his fingers drift over her wet panties. "You're drenched," he said on a low growl.

"I need to come." Raising her hips, she attempted to gain more pressure, and he gave it to her, rubbing over her panties, pressing down, and moving his palm in small circles.

He moved the material to the side, coating his fingers with her juices and pushing one digit inside. "Better?"

"Yes," she said, trembling until he began to pump his finger in and out of her sex, rubbing her inner walls as he moved. "I'm close," she whimpered.

He squeezed his legs around her at the same time he curled his finger inside. "Come for me, Samantha." He slid his finger out of her body and pressed down on her clit.

She detonated, her body stiffening against him. "Dex!"

He circled faster and she rocked her hips, rubbing her sex against his hand, her moans filling the night, the movie long forgotten.

Lifting her, he placed her beside him, pulled a condom from his wallet, shedding his jeans and boxer briefs. He rolled on protection and sat back down beside her.

He looked at her flushed face and dazed expression, her eyelids heavy, and knew she had more in her. "Come here."

She pulled off her panties and rose to her knees, then straddled his lap. Taking his cock in her hand, she placed it at her entrance, then slid down, enclosing him in warm heat.

He closed his eyes, soaking in the feel of being squeezed inside her. He groaned at the same time she did and she met his gaze. "So good," she said in a sexy voice. "I'm so full."

"Take us over," he instructed, and she began to rise and fall, rocking her sex against him with each joining of their bodies. Her movements came faster, more frantic, and suddenly he felt her spasm around his dick, triggering a climax of his own.

He wasn't sure how long he stayed inside her before he finally came to his senses. Her dress floated around them, providing coverage, not that anyone was around to watch.

"Up," he said, and she climbed off.

They did their best to pull themselves together. He tied off the condom, wrapped it in a napkin, and tossed it in the trash while she picked up her panties and made a face.

"I can't wear my underwear again," she said, blushing. "It's too wet."

He chuckled. "I take pride in that." Grabbing the

scrap of material, he shoved it into his jeans pocket.

Not meeting his gaze, she gathered her hair and put it up in a messy bun.

"Samantha."

She looked over and said, "We just had sex outside." As if she'd just realized what they'd done.

He touched beneath her chin. "Nobody saw," he assured her. Leaning forward, he kissed her lips, something he should have made sure to do earlier. "Want to watch the rest of the movie?"

She shook her head. "Do you mind if we leave? I'm kind of a mess."

He took in her wild hair and the makeup smeared beneath her eyes. She was every bit as sexy as when he'd picked her up. Even more, he thought.

"You're still gorgeous but we can do whatever you want. Come on." He clasped her hand. "Let's go home and shower."

She swallowed hard. "Only if we do it together." She said the words and dipped her head.

But he grinned at her mix of sassy shyness. "That's my girl."

Her lips turned downward at the expression he'd casually tossed out. "Dex, remember what I said about my crazy life?"

Fuck. The last thing he wanted to do was scare her off. Reminding himself of what he'd learned about her, that she needed someone to give her what she needed, he swallowed a groan. "I remember. We're doing this at your speed." He paused. "As long as we're doing this."

She didn't reply but when they returned to her apartment, she pulled him inside and he spent the night.

# Chapter Fourteen

S AMANTHA SAT IN the conference room of Drake Blakely, Esq., listening to Tim Daley, the lawyer she'd hired, read the list of Jeremy's demands before he would even consider dissolving the partnership, which included him taking their top clients.

"A buyout is off the table?" she asked, horrified.

"It's a tactic," Tim, her lawyer, assured her.

"You mean he'll want an obscene amount of money to go away," she muttered.

Tim, a middle-aged man with a receding hairline and a large stomach, sat at the head of the table. "Probably, but I have maneuvers of my own. I suggest we stall him by bringing in a forensic accountant to go over the books."

"Are you concerned?"

"Irrelevant," Tim said with a shrug. "It's standard when dissolving a business or prior to a buyout. But considering Jeremy was willing to marry you and play the long game to get his hands on your money, once we inform him of the plan, he's going to panic and we might see whether or not he's operating on the up and up."

She blinked, stunned at what he was insinuating. "You think he's stealing from the business?"

"I've seen these situations before and I wouldn't be surprised. Stay calm and work as usual. I'll handle the rest. If he approaches you about things, refer him to me."

Her stomach twisted as she rose from her seat. "Thank you, Tim."

"My pleasure. Don't worry, Samantha. I've handled worse snakes than your partner."

She managed a smile but was happy she had this man in her corner.

"I'll be in touch," he said. "In the meantime, it's business as usual for you."

With a nod, she walked out of the conference room. Once she was in the hall by the elevators, she pulled out her phone and texted Dex, letting him know she'd left and would meet him at his brother's bar as planned. She pulled up a rideshare app and waited on the corner.

By the time she arrived at the bar, she'd worked herself up over how Jeremy might react when he found out she'd hired the forensic accountant. Dex met her outside the back door, which was the main entrance and accounted for the bar's name.

She walked into his embrace and relaxed for the first time.

As he wrapped his strong arms around her, she knew she was getting in deep with this man. At the moment, she couldn't bring herself to care.

"What happened at the lawyer's?" he asked.

Stepping back, she met his gaze. "We went over Jeremy's list of wants in order to dissolve the partnership." She enumerated them for Dex as they entered the bar. "He says a total buyout is off the table but Tim, my lawyer, says it's just a tactic."

"More attempts to get his hands on your money," Dex said in a low, angry voice.

"Exactly."

"Hi, brother-in-law!" Raven walked over with menus in hand and kissed Dex's cheek. "Table for two?"

"Yes," he said. "Samantha, this is Remy's wife, Raven. Raven, meet Samantha Dare."

"Aah, Samantha. It's a pleasure to meet you," the pretty woman said. "I admit to being curious."

Dex narrowed his gaze. "Raven, behave."

Samantha blushed but coming from a large family, she understood. "If my brother disappeared with a woman in a wedding dress, I'd be curious too." Might as well mention the elephant in the room, Samantha thought.

Raven laughed. "I like you. Come on. Let me get you two settled."

A few minutes later, they had their soft drinks and instead of being alone, Raven had joined them. Then Remy, Dex's brother, walked out from the back offices. Introductions were made and they started talking about how Raven and Remy went from boss and employee to husband and wife. Samantha enjoyed hearing their story.

"Remy is not just a bar owner, he's a private investigator," Dex said, placing his hand over hers. In public.

She shivered at his touch and Raven gave her a knowing look. The type that said, *I know you have feelings for my brother-in-law.* She wouldn't be wrong.

"You know, maybe we should have him look into Jeremy," Dex suggested.

Remy turned toward her. "I'm happy to do it. What do you think?"

She liked that Remy asked her opinion, that he didn't just jump to do what Dex suggested.

"Samantha?" Dex asked.

She liked more that Dex asked her, too. He didn't just decide and trample over her choices like Ian might have done in the same situation.

"I appreciate it but I think I'll let things play out with my lawyer, at least for now." She didn't want Tim to feel as though she were undermining him or his work. He had a plan and she'd stick with it.

Remy nodded. "If you need me, I'm here."

She smiled, liking Dex's brother. "Thanks again."

A few minutes later, a dark-haired woman in a flowing skirt walked in and pulled a chair over to the table. "Thanks for letting me know to stop by," she said to Raven before turning to Samantha. "Hi, I'm Dex's only sister. Fallon." She treated Samantha to a smile.

"Hi."

"What the hell is going on?" Dex asked, glaring at his sister-in-law.

She shrugged and glanced at Remy. "Remy and I thought the rest of the family would like to meet Samantha."

"Don't you think a heads-up would be nice?" He glared at them both while Samantha's cheeks burned.

He turned toward her. "We can leave. I'm sure the last thing you expected on an already stressful day was to be ambushed by my family."

She shook her head. "It's fine. I come from a huge clan, remember? I just don't want them to think we're more serious than we really are," she whispered, finding it hard to meet his gaze.

The last thing she wanted to do was hurt him and as she spoke, the words felt wrong on her tongue. But she refused to put herself in a position where she was in a relationship again so soon.

"It's all good." He squeezed her hand in reassurance. "Fallon, what's up with you?" Dex changed the subject and focused on his sister.

"The store next to the gallery closed and instead of leasing it to someone else, Clara is going to run with my idea to join it with the gallery so we can have classes and parties, along with some wine drinking. I want to call it Paint, Party & Sip." She clasped her hands together, her excitement obvious. "It's mostly for adults but I can accommodate older teens, too."

"That sounds fun," Samantha said. "I'd love to give it a try."

"I'll be sure to let you know when we're open." Fallon beamed at the prospect, her cheeks flushed and eyes bright.

Remy's phone rang and he answered, talking for a few seconds before hanging up. "Well, Jared and Aiden can't get away from the office because Dad went home early."

Dex frowned. "Is he not feeling well?" Beside her, he stiffened and Samantha noticed Fallon reacted similarly.

"Damned if I know. He's stubborn. Refuses to slow down like the doctors ordered him to do. I think Lizzie is frustrated and concerned."

Fallon sighed. "I already tried to talk to him. Maybe if one of you did too?"

"I've got it," Dex said. "I'll take a ride over there in the next day or so."

Samantha placed a hand on his shoulder. Though she didn't know what was going on, he was obviously worried and as much as he'd been a support for her, she wanted to do the same in return.

"Let me know how you make out," Remy said. "Maybe if Raven and I go after you, he'll get the message."

The mood lightened up after the talk about their father and another hour passed by the time everyone stood to leave.

After saying goodbye to his family, Dex turned to face her. "How are you getting home?"

"Uber," she said, opening her bag to search for her phone.

"I've got you. My car is parked in the lot."

"Are you sure? I don't mind taking a rideshare," she said, not wanting him to have to go out of his way.

"I mind." He tapped her nose. "Come on. This way I can spend a little more time with you."

Warmth filled her, both at his offer and reason.

Once they were settled inside the vehicle and on their way, she turned toward him. "I really like your family."

"They're nosey," he said but his voice held a hint of affection.

She laughed. "Because they love you. I'm sure that's why they wanted to check me out."

"I love them too. Even when I want to kill them," he muttered. "But I'm glad you didn't mind the ambush."

"Of course not. My family would do the same thing."

He didn't reply and she had a weird feeling about his silence. "Dex? Is something wrong?"

He kept one hand on the wheel, eyes on the road, but he grabbed her hand with his free one. "I've been debating when to explain this to you. Since we're talking about protective family members, this is probably as good a time as any."

She kicked off her heel and curled the leg beneath her, turning to face him. "What did Ian do?" she asked, because it didn't take a perceptive genius to figure out this had something to do with her overprotective brother.

"Remember you mentioned that I pulled away from kissing you twice?"

She nodded. "I do," she said, her stomach suddenly in knots.

"That New Year's Eve night with you was life-altering. You were smart and sexy. That whole evening was special. But after the kiss, I turned my head and saw Ian glaring at me. At the time, I was a rookie and he held my career in his hands." She heard the regret in his voice.

"I understand why you backed off, but I don't get why my brother thought it was okay to mess with my life." She'd been so into Dex, so swept off her feet by the man. His turning cold on her had hurt badly.

He pulled in front of her building, put the vehicle in park, and turned to meet her gaze. "The same reason Fallon came today. He loves you and was protective. You were young. I was football focused."

She curled her hands into fists. "It wasn't his place."

He cupped a hand beneath her chin. "Maybe it was, maybe it wasn't, but he did us a favor. I needed to focus on my career and couldn't make you a priority. I can now."

She swallowed hard. "But—"

"But nothing. You asked for time, you have time. You need to get your life in order, I respect that. But I'm no longer a kid who'll listen to another man telling me what to do. You're the only one who has a say in this relationship. Not my family or yours." He slid his hand around her neck and pulled her toward him, sealing his lips over hers.

He took her like he'd done that night under the mistletoe, showing her he meant what he said. This time, he wasn't going anywhere. Every nerve ending inside her ignited, her body aflame. She moaned into his mouth. Wrapped her arms around his neck and let the kiss go on until he pulled back, out of breath.

He touched his forehead to hers. "Go inside before I can't control myself." His low growl turned her on even more.

Though they'd spent a good amount of time together, she'd been forcing herself to have alone time to think. So she didn't jump into something so soon after Jeremy. As much as she wanted to invite him up, she forced herself to open the car door and walk into her building alone.

# Chapter Fifteen

THE NEXT MORNING, Dex woke up and before he showered for the day, he called his dad's cell. Better to know what he was in for today prior to getting ready.

To his surprise, Lizzie answered. "Hello?"

"Hi, Lizzie. It's Dex. How are you?"

"I'm fine, sweetheart. I know you called your dad but he's outside on a ladder changing a light bulb above the garage," she said.

Dex pinched the bridge of his nose. "What happened to the handyman you hired to fix some things around the house to make Dad's life easier?"

"Your father said—"

"He can do it himself," they repeated at the same time.

Dex groaned. "Listen, is it okay if I come over in a couple of hours?" Obviously, this was the perfect time to talk to his dad about his and his siblings' concerns about his heart and overdoing activity.

"Of course," Lizzie said. "Oh! Bring that lovely girl, Samantha, that Fallon told me about. Your father and I want to meet her."

Dex hesitated then realized his dad might take the criticism better if he brought Samantha and just mentioned his concerns rather than confronting him straight out.

"I'll see if she's free to come."

"Wonderful! Let me know and if she can, I'll make lunch." Her voice rose in excitement. "And, Dex?"

"Yes?" he asked.

"I know you're coming to talk to your father, and I appreciate it. I'm so worried about him."

Knowing he was doing the right thing, the vise squeezing Dex's chest eased. "We're all worried. It's my turn to try and make him see reason."

"Thank you," she murmured.

They said their goodbyes and he called Samantha. He was about to hang up, disappointed, when he heard her voice. "Dex!" she panted his name.

"Hey, beautiful. Am I interrupting something?"

"I just got out of the shower. What's up?" she asked, obviously unaware she'd just put visions of water dripping over her perfect skin into his head.

He cleared his throat and adjusted his cock in his boxer briefs. "I wondered if you wanted to take a ride to my father's house in Old Brookville. I need to talk to my dad and could use the moral support."

"You're going to talk to your father about pushing too hard, aren't you?" she asked.

"Yeah. When I called earlier he was up on a ladder changing an outdoor garage light." He cringed at the thought of what could have happened if he'd fallen.

"Oh no!" Samantha said. "Of course I'll come with you. I'm sure it won't be easy to remind him he needs to slow down. What time should I be ready?"

He breathed out a sigh of relief. The conversation wouldn't be easy and having her there would help. "Thanks, beautiful. I'll pick you up around eleven. It takes about an hour and ten minutes without traffic. Lizzie, my dad's girlfriend, said she'd make lunch."

"Great. Can we stop on the way so I can pick up dessert?" Samantha asked.

"Sure thing," he said.

His father and Lizzie were going to love her.

THE LONG RIDE to Dex's father's house gave Samantha plenty of time to overthink. Of course, she wanted to be his emotional support while talking to his dad about slowing down. No man, or woman for that matter, wanted to hear they couldn't keep up with their normal activities. She understood why Dex was hesitant about the conversation.

Samantha worried about meeting his father and girlfriend. Being by his side and supporting him through something so emotional might lead them to assume she and Dex were a couple. But a friend would definitely be by Dex's side, too, and that's how she had to think of them.

Dex pulled up to a beautiful home set far back from the road. An explosion of peonies, petunias, hydrangeas, and other flowers Samantha couldn't name brought a variety of pinks to life outside the house between the green shrubbery.

"Here we are." He gestured with one arm as he cut the engine.

"It's beautiful." The massive colonial house was nothing like her mother's Florida home because theirs was a pale yellow stucco but it was equally as large.

She could imagine Dex and his siblings roughhousing on the front lawn… and then remembered they'd moved here at least three or four years after their mom died, having lived with their father's parents while Alexander Sterling grieved the loss of his wife, and the kids their mother. But there were four boys, so she decided they'd definitely played around on this grass or in the backyard she hadn't yet seen.

"Come on. I'm sure Lizzie's waiting." He climbed out and walked around to her side, opening the door and extending a hand to help her out.

Together, they strode up the path to the front door where a pretty woman and a good-looking man met them on the outside porch.

"Dex! It's good to see you." His father stepped forward and pulled him into a hug, patting him on the back.

"Hey, Dad." Dex stepped back. "Lizzie," he said, kissing the woman on the cheek. "This is Samantha Dare." Reaching back, Dex clasped her hand and pulled her parallel with him.

"It's nice to meet you both," Samantha said. "I brought a cake from my favorite bakery." She extended the box and Lizzie accepted it.

"Perfect! We'll have some after lunch. Though you didn't need to come with anything. You taking the trip here with Dex is enough."

Lizzie held the cake in one hand and hooked an arm into Samantha's. "We're going to the kitchen. You two hang out. I'll call you when lunch is ready," she said.

Samantha walked through the house, taking in the modern feel. Along the way to the kitchen, she passed gorgeous canvas paintings with pops of stark color that stood out. "I love these," she said, pointing to one in particular.

"Oh, Fallon made that one along with all the others hanging in the house. You should stop by the gallery where she works and check out her paintings," Lizzie said with pride. Though Fallon wasn't her daughter, it was clear Lizzie considered her family.

Once they were settled in the kitchen, a room large enough to cook for and hold the whole family, Lizzie pulled up a chair by the table and invited Samantha to sit.

"I hope you don't mind that I pulled you in here. I want Dex to have time to talk to Alex about overdoing things," Lizzie said.

Samantha shook her head. "Of course not. Dex told me he needed to have a word with his dad."

"I don't know if Dex mentioned it, but his father had a mild heart attack almost one year ago and the doctors warned Alex about his diet and activity. He's supposed to do mild walking and exercise but he doesn't understand the word *mild*. He's been going to work most days and staying late. The man's going to give me a heart attack if he doesn't relax," Lizzie said with a chuckle but Samantha sensed the seriousness behind the words.

"Can I get you something to drink?" Lizzie asked.

"No, thanks. I'm fine for now."

Lizzie rose to her feet. "Well, I could use a glass of ice water. I'm thirsty." She walked to a cabinet and took out a glass, then filled it with water at the Sub-Zero fridge. "Dex tells me you're from a large family, too?"

"Oh, yes. I grew up with five siblings. Three

brothers and two sisters." She debated going further then decided, why not? "I also have three half-siblings."

"Well, then. The size of this table isn't a shock for you."

She laughed. "Not at all."

Lizzie grew silent and Samantha assumed she was worrying about what Dex was saying to his dad.

DEX FOLLOWED HIS father through the house and out the back door to the pool deck in the backyard. Alex sat down on his favorite recliner and Dex pulled up a chair next to him, looking out over the hedges separating their property from the neighbors'.

"Right through that hedge is the path where I used to sneak through to come over." His parents would be arguing and nobody would realize a five-year-old was missing until Gloria called and let them know.

His father laughed. "Gloria always set an extra seat for you."

Dex leaned forward, hands clasped together. "You have no idea how much I appreciated it."

"I think I do." His father met his gaze, a serious look in his eyes.

This was his chance. "You've always been there for

me and I'm grateful."

His father slapped his knee. "Because you're as much my son as Remy, Aiden, or Jared."

"And we love you and don't want to lose you before it's time because you're too stubborn to listen to your doctor." He swiped his sunglasses off his head and placed them over his eyes.

Alex was a good-looking, strong, and solidly built man, who didn't look at all like he'd had a heart attack last year. Which was probably why he found it difficult to listen to the cardiologist and relax more. Despite his health scare.

"Lizzie and your sister worry too much."

"It's not just the women, Dad. We're all worried about you. We saw you in the hospital bed and you were weak, and it scared us. You have control of your future. Just listen to the doctors, dammit." Dex braced his hands on the arms of the chair and rose, shoving the seat back.

He paced the patio, sweating beneath the sun, trying to decide whether or not his father deserved for him to pull out the emotional big guns. So to speak.

"Son, do you have any idea what it's like to be monitored? To feel like a child being told what I can and cannot do because I'm getting older?"

Dex drew a deep breath. "Not exactly. But I know what it's like to have to retire when my body can't keep up with the younger players and I know what it's like to lose my parents. Then my second mother. And I do not want to lose you just because you're being stubborn or feeling like a child. Nobody can handle that loss, Dad. Not when it's preventable!" The words exploded from him and he couldn't bring himself to regret them.

Alex sucked in a shocked breath, then pushed himself to his feet. "Dex."

Turning, he faced the man who'd raised him, was the role model he'd needed since he was a young boy, and most of all, who loved him. "I should have been nicer about how I said that. But you know it's true."

Alex walked over and put an arm around his shoulders. "Point made. I'll watch myself."

Dex nodded, his shoulders sagging in relief. "While we're putting truths out there, I have a question. Something I've been wondering since my parents' accident."

"What is it?"

He ran a hand over his face. "I heard the police talking that night. About the witness who said my mother was reaching for the steering wheel?"

"Damn."

"I ran before I could hear more and drew my own conclusions. Were they arguing? Is that what the witness saw?" Maybe if he asked, he could avoid those nightmares in the future.

"Let's sit."

He followed his father back to the chairs and they took their seats. "Yes. The woman who witnessed the accident said it looked like the couple was arguing, but let's face it. She wasn't in the vehicle. She couldn't be sure."

Dex shook his head. "They were definitely fighting. There wasn't a time when they weren't. Why do you think I came here so often before they passed away?" He gestured to the hedges. "I needed the peace I found here. Even with all the kids, it was a happy loudness I didn't find at home."

"I'm glad we could give you that. Even before you became ours."

"So give me something. And I know you've already given me everything, but I'm asking for one more thing when it comes to your health and well-being."

He smiled and shook his head. "I'll take care of myself, son. I'll change my habits and listen to the doctors. I promise."

Dex let out a relieved, long breath. "Thanks, Dad. That means the world." He couldn't wait to text his siblings to relieve their stress, too.

He wondered if it was ironic that it was the adopted son who'd gotten through to Alex, then shook his head. He was just as much a Sterling as any of his other brothers or Fallon. He just happened to have the right words at the right time.

"Why don't we go inside and enjoy Lizzie's lunch. I'm sure it's healthy."

Dex chuckled. "I'm sure you'll be thrilled to know Samantha brought a heart-healthy carrot cake." He rose from his seat and glanced at his dad. "And no, you cannot have it à la mode."

"I suppose I should get used to hearing things like that." Alex sighed and they headed back to the house.

# Chapter Sixteen

A FEW DAYS later, Dex woke up to his phone vibrating like mad. If not for a business dinner last night, he'd have stayed over at Samantha's, but work came first. He'd been out late with the producers of his Sunday night TV broadcast, having a steak dinner and discussing the upcoming season. He planned to travel to Kansas City about five days prior to the first game and they'd begin interviewing the players and coaches.

Reaching for his phone, he sat up in bed and glanced at his notifications, his stomach sinking at the posts from TNZ. "Oh, shit."

Someone had taken photos of him and Samantha outside The Back Door after her meeting with the lawyer. She'd been upset and he'd been consoling her. She'd been cuddled up to his side with his arm around her.

*Is pro playboy, and former Miami Thunder quarterback, Dex Sterling, a home-wrecker? The upcoming* Sunday Night Football *commentator who recently signed a multimillion-dollar deal with FSN was seen in an intimate, midday embrace outside The Back Door, his brother's SoHo bar. Was the runaway bride two-timing her fiancé?*

Their hug had been twisted into something ugly. Just like his agent had feared. But he wasn't worried about himself. He was concerned about Samantha.

Austin had called three times and a glimpse at the comments on the post showed Dex being called a home-wrecker and Samantha much worse. All because the news didn't have the accurate story about her leaving her cheating, lying fiancé at the altar. And because the truth wouldn't make for salacious news about FSN's new hire.

The phone rang and he glanced at the screen. "Goddammit." He couldn't ignore it and took the call. "Ian."

"What the fuck?"

Dex rubbed a palm over his pounding forehead. "We both know it's bullshit and it'll blow over by the next scandal. Have you spoken to your sister?"

"She's not answering. If you need me to get my lawyers on this, let me know."

Dex blinked. That was a lot better than Ian yelling at him for not taking care of Samantha. "If it'd help, I'd do that myself, but thanks. TNZ didn't outright say I did anything, they asked if I did. Which gives them leeway they don't deserve," he muttered, hopping out of bed. "I'm going to your sister's place in a few minutes. I just woke up to this clusterfuck."

"Call me if you need anything." Ian disconnected the call.

Before he did anything, he typed out a text on the family chat, letting them know he was okay and handling things. Then he took a quick shower and dressed for the day.

Once he was in his Benz, he pulled out of the lot, only to realize there were paparazzi on the sidewalk. Dammit. He was used to them on the rare red carpet he walked and when he was introduced as the face of FSN. But never with the kind of negative press he was receiving now.

On the way uptown to Samantha's, he called Austin and let his agent yell. It wouldn't change anything but it would let the man get it out and calm down. Once he did, Austin begged him to lay low and not go out in public with Samantha, at least for now, leaving Austin cursing again. But he did express concern for his cousin and the press that might be following her. That was the only reason he wasn't furious with him asking Dex to hide his relationship with Samantha. The one she thought was a close friendship and he considered much more. In the end, Austin promised he'd do his job, meaning damage control on Dex's behalf.

Finally, he pulled up to Samantha's building, frustrated to see the paparazzi there, too, on the public sidewalk. Ignoring their shouting, he left his vehicle with the doorman who promised to keep an eye on it.

Samantha had put him on her permanent guest list and he took the elevator to her apartment. He knocked and waited for her to answer, hoping she wasn't furious with him for putting her front and center before the tabloids.

He heard the sound of her unlocking the door and it swung open. Samantha stood before him in her work clothes, a gorgeous vision in a pencil skirt and white V-neck blouse. She wore makeup and did not have the look of a woman whose life had been wrecked again. But she didn't look happy, either, not that he blamed her.

"Dex! I'm so sorry." She stepped aside so he could walk in.

Her words confused him but he waited until she shut and locked the door before asking, "Sorry for what?"

"Those pictures and the text," she said anxiously. "I don't have anything that could be affected but I know the network is going to be upset with those photos. I dragged you into my mess from the beginning and I'm beyond sorry. Should you even be here now? The doorman told me there are paparazzi outside."

"You have nothing to be sorry for. I'm with you

because I want to be."

"I know but being my friend shouldn't cause problems for you," she murmured, a frown furrowing her brow.

Ignoring the discussion of their relationship status, her earlier words buzzed around his brain. He couldn't figure out how she knew the network would care one way or another and suddenly realization dawned. "Austin. Did he call you?" he asked of his agent and her *cousin*.

She pulled her lush bottom lip between her teeth. "Well, to be fair, most of my family called this morning. When TNZ posts, it usually goes viral."

Dex walked over and braced his hands on her hips. "Listen to me. As far as I'm concerned, we're in this together."

And he'd keep being there. That was the only way he could prove to her he was worth trying another relationship because he wasn't going anywhere.

She stepped closer and then she was in his arms, hugging him tight, the tension in her body ebbing. "Thank you. But your career—"

"My character speaks for itself," he interrupted her, his tone gruff. "If they don't like it, they can shove their morality clause up their asses and I'll sue."

Despite the seriousness of the conversation, he felt her laughter against his chest. "You're special, Dex."

She glanced up at him and he tipped his head, pressing his lips to hers… but not for long.

He wanted nothing more than to mess her up, smear her red lipstick, and take her against the wall, fucking her until her eyes teared and she came hard. But she was dressed for work and had obviously put time and effort into her appearance, no doubt due to everything going on around them, so he stepped back.

"Can I give you a ride to work?"

She smiled and nodded. "Before we walk out together, are you *sure*?"

"Dead sure." He held out a hand and she placed her palm in his, confirming they were a team.

PRETENDING TO BE fine in front of Dex hadn't been easy but she'd been doing it since the wedding. Nobody needed to see her fall apart. Despite her own emotional issues courtesy of her upcoming discussion with Jeremy that was bound to turn into an argument over the forensic accountant, and splitting up, or her buying out the business, today was about Dex. He was the one with a career at stake because of her life choices and he needed her support this time, not the other way around. The truth was, her stomach was churning, she was nauseous, and she hadn't been able to eat anything today.

Samantha had been running on fumes since her wedding. Nerves that day had spiraled into a daily state of anxiety, something she'd kept to herself. She didn't want anyone worrying about her more than they already were. Not even Dex knew how upset she was over the conversation she needed to have with Jeremy.

By the time Dex dropped her off at the building where her office was located, she'd grown dizzy but shook it off and chalked the feeling up to the ever-present anxiety. Today's was worse, as men and women with cameras were waiting outside of both her apartment and work, standing on the sidewalk, snapping photos of her as she exited the car. It was so bad, Dex walked her to the doors, shielding her with his big body. Once inside, she'd insisted on heading upstairs alone.

She needed space to think because she understood the problem, even if Dex refused to see it. Them being together only fed the gossip and gave the paparazzi more to write about. She wasn't a household name but for sports fans and women who followed hot athletes, Dex was well known. Add in his new contract and name in sports media, and his being with her made for juicy headlines and could possibly put his new job at risk.

Her cousin and Dex's agent, Austin, wasn't pleased

with their relationship. He'd warned her that they both had something to lose but she could only see the downside for Dex and promised herself she'd pull back. Something Dex made difficult for her to do because he was always there for her in every way.

She stepped off the elevator and right into Jeremy.

"Just the person I wanted to see," he said, approaching her with anger in his narrowed gaze. "How dare you embarrass me by hooking up with another man so soon after our broken engagement. It's public and humiliating!"

Anger welled up inside her at the audacity of the man. "Are you kidding? Just because you weren't caught publicly doesn't mean you aren't responsible for things ending. Don't try and twist things around, Jeremy. I'm short on patience this morning and you're the last person I want to see." She turned to go and he grabbed her arm, spinning her around to face him again.

"Don't walk out on me. We weren't finished. You've been ignoring my calls and my texts about the business." His face grew red with anger and she swallowed hard, jerking back her arm.

"Get your fucking hands off me and if you have a problem with my decisions about the business, talk to my lawyer."

He narrowed his gaze. "Do you really think bringing in some outside forensic accountant is going to stop me from getting what's mine? *I* built this business," he said, his voice rising.

Oh no, he did not just say that. "*We* built this business and don't you forget it," she said, straightening her shoulders.

She wasn't going to cower even if his fury *was* reminding her of that moment in her apartment when he struck her.

She glanced around but it wasn't yet nine a.m. and they seemed to be alone.

He stepped closer and she backed herself against the nearest wall. "Move away," she said in the sternest voice she could manage. Black spots flickered in front of her eyes. Dammit. She should have eaten something earlier.

"Hey! Get the fuck away from her!" Brandy rushed over and grabbed Samantha's arm, pulling her from Jeremy who was looming over her. She stumbled toward her friend, grateful for her timing.

"Fucking bitch," Jeremy yelled, before storming off in the direction of his office.

"I'm dizzy," Samantha said, and Brandy immediately wrapped an arm around her waist and led her to a chair at the nearest desk.

Brandy knelt down, worry in her eyes. "What's going on? Do you need me to call 911?"

Samantha ran her tongue over her dry lips, her head spinning. "I'm sure it's low blood sugar because I didn't eat this morning."

Brandy pursed her lips. With determination, she said, "That's it. I'm taking you home."

Because Samantha felt like crap, she didn't argue. She rose to her feet and immediately felt herself going down as she blacked out.

LATER THAT DAY, Dex met his brother Jared at the gym near his apartment. The paparazzi had left his residence, allowing him to walk there. He worked out, showered at the gym, and after, they walked outside. The plan was for him and Jared to head downtown for drinks, to talk and catch up. Since their dad's heart attack, Jared had been working overtime at the office, trying to do things that would take the heavy lifting off their father's plate.

"Want me to drive us to The Back Door?" Dex asked.

Jared shrugged. "Let's Uber. We're going to have to come back uptown after. No need to go get your car from the lot." He pulled out his phone to request a rideshare.

While waiting, Dex called Samantha to say hello.

The phone rang and a familiar female voice answered. "Hi, Dex. It's Brandy," Samantha's friend said.

"Hey. Is Samantha there?" Or was she too bogged down with work to talk, he wondered.

"She can't come to the phone right now but… hang on." He heard rustling, and then, "I'm back. Dex, Samantha's in the hospital."

His stomach churned at her words. "What happened? What's wrong?"

"She had an argument with that asshole and passed out."

"What?!" Dex drew a deep breath, getting control of his anger, and his worry. "Did he touch her?" His heart threatened to beat out of his chest.

"Yeah. After, she was dizzy and I had her sit down. Once she was better, I helped her stand… and she passed out cold. But she woke up pretty quickly."

He blew out a long breath.

"She said she just hadn't eaten today," Brandy went on. "But I insisted she go to the hospital anyway. Someone called 911. She's fine but I thought you'd want to know."

"Are you there with her now?" he asked.

"Yes."

"Which hospital?"

The question had Jared staring in concern. Dex held up a hand. He needed answers before he could explain things to his brother.

He waited for Brandy to give him the name and Samantha's location. "I'll be there as soon as I can." He disconnected the call and turned to Jared. "It's Samantha," he said. "She's at Sinai, so I'm heading over. Sorry. We'll catch up later?"

Jared slapped his shoulder. "Of course. Shoot me a text and let me know she's okay."

"Will do." Dex stepped to the curb and held out a hand to hail an empty taxi, lucky to get one right away.

By the time he arrived at the ER, his need for answers had grown. At least Brandy had said Samantha was okay, but that wasn't enough until he laid eyes on her himself.

He walked in and saw Brandy in the hallway outside a sliding glass door to an ER room and strode over. "How is she?"

"Okay. They're giving her fluids for dehydration. Come on in. She's going to be furious I told you."

He frowned at that. "Well, I'd be the furious one if I'd been left in the dark."

Brandy looked at him and smirked. "Well, we wouldn't want that. Samantha needs you, whether she wants to admit it or not," she said, grasping his arm. "Samantha, I hope you're decent because you have company!" Brandy spoke in a singsong voice as she pulled him into the hospital room.

# Chapter Seventeen

S AMANTHA LAY IN the hospital bed, hooked up to an IV bag dripping fluids into her. A well-meaning nurse had given her a scolding about staying hydrated and taking better care of herself, adding to her feeling ridiculous for being in here in the first place. They'd brought her a turkey sandwich, Jell-O, and a plastic cup of apple juice, which she'd devoured, and the food had done wonders for her energy level, headache, and spots in front of her eyes. She felt better already.

She couldn't believe she'd fainted in the office. It wasn't something she was prone to, but she'd been under so much stress lately, and thinking about eating usually made her queasy. The confrontation with Jeremy hadn't helped the situation, either.

"Do you want me to call anyone?" Brandy asked from the chair at the end of the bed.

Samantha shook her head. "You've been such a good friend, meeting me here and staying while they run tests and lecture me."

Brandy chuckled. "You scared me to death when you went down."

Feeling her cheeks flame at the reminder, Samantha groaned.

"Listen, I have to ask… is there any chance you're pregnant? Because when my cousin Patti was pregnant, she was a fainter." Brandy raised her eyebrows in question.

Though her stomach did a somersault at the question, Samantha shook her head. "I really don't think so." She and Dex used condoms and after the nightmare with Jeremy, she'd gone to her doctor to get tested and then opted to take the pill, too. Though it was too soon for that to have kicked in. Just to be safe. "I just couldn't handle any more upheaval in my life, so it's highly unlikely."

"Okay." Brandy's shoulders slumped in relief. "They said they'd have the blood work back in an hour, but I had to ask."

Samantha managed a smile and before she could say anything else, her cell rang.

Brandy glanced down and grabbed the phone from its place on the bed before Samantha could look. "You rest. I'll make sure nobody bothers you." With a pointed look, she walked outside.

Samantha listened but all she could hear was her friend's muted voice, too low to hear. Assuming it was work, she turned on the television. *TNZ LIVE* was already on and in case there was something about Dex and his job, she settled in to watch news about celebrities.

Her friend rejoined her in the room.

"Who was on the phone?" Samantha asked.

"Brian was checking on you. What's on television?" she asked, sitting back down in the chair. She looked up at the screen while Samantha raised the volume on the remote.

After a little while, she began to doze off.

"That bastard!" Brandy said, startling Samantha, and she jerked in bed. "Turn up the volume!"

A glance up and she saw Jeremy on the screen outside their office building. Her stomach rolled and she raised the volume along with holding up the remote/speaker so she could hear better.

"I'm disappointed that Dex Sterling would get in between a man and his future wife. I've been dismayed and hurt ever since Samantha left me at the altar, and now I know why she did it." Though Jeremy spoke to an interviewer, the gleam in his eye was all for Samantha.

"I hate him!" she yelled, attempting to throw the remote only to remember a thick wire tethered it to the bed.

"Calm down," Brandy said, "or you'll have the staff come running."

Samantha blew out a long breath. "You're right. Letting him get to me is how I ended up here in the first place."

"Can I get you something? Maybe they have tea here. I'll go ask."

Wanting a few minutes alone, she didn't argue with her friend.

Brandy walked out and Samantha closed her eyes, determined to stay calm. She wasn't sure how much time had passed when she heard Brandy's singsong voice drifting toward her.

"Samantha, I hope you're decent because you have a visitor!" Brandy pulled Dex into the room. "Sorry I didn't get your tea. I ran into company."

At the sound of Dex's voice, she looked toward the door. "What are you doing here?" she asked, turning to a grinning Brandy.

"I called and your friend told me where you were." He tipped his chin at Brandy. "What did the doctors say?"

Brandy picked up her purse. "She's getting fluids, bloodwork will be back soon, and she needs to eat, hydrate, and reduce stress. I'm going back to the office to keep an eye on your partner."

"Don't engage," Dex warned, and Brandy nodded as she waved and strode out.

He walked toward Samantha and sat down beside her, taking her hand. She curled her fingers and was forced to admit him being here made everything better.

"How are you feeling?" he asked.

"Better. They've been feeding me and not just through this." She held up her free hand with the IV attached. "I'm mortified that I passed out."

"We'll talk about you not eating later. What happened with Jeremy this morning?" he asked, just as the doctor walked into the room.

"Ms. Dare? I have your bloodwork and everything is normal. As soon as the IV finishes, the nurse can take it out and we'll discharge you. How are you feeling?"

"Much better, thank you." She smiled at the man who'd been pleasant all morning.

"My pleasure. Now, for discharge instructions. Take it easy today. Make sure to eat and not let yourself get so empty your blood sugar and blood pressure drops, okay?"

She nodded, her cheeks heating at the reminder she shouldn't need.

"In general, those are doctor's orders. Also avoid stress. Do you have any questions?"

"No. Thank you."

Once they were alone again, Dex met her gaze. "Okay, beautiful. New rules. I'm taking you home and I'm staying for a couple of days until I'm sure you're not too dizzy to be alone."

"You're going to babysit me, aren't you?"

He rose until he loomed over her, placing a hand on top of the bed and leaning down until they were nose to nose. "I'm going to watch over every inch of you." His voice held a promise she couldn't wait for him to fulfill.

DEX TOOK SAMANTHA home from the hospital in an Uber and once they were upstairs, she lay down on the sofa and put on a romantic comedy. He took one look in her cabinets and sat down to order in groceries and the ingredients for lasagna.

By the time he'd put the food away and prepped dinner, including garlic bread, and rejoined Samantha in the living room, she'd fallen asleep.

He was beyond concerned about her. It wasn't just how frazzled she must be to forget to eat but he still didn't know what happened when Jeremy confronted her. If the man touched her again, he was going to show him what it meant to be hit by an ex-pro football player.

He glanced over and her eyes fluttered open. "I can't believe I fell asleep," she said, pushing herself back against the thick armrest. He adjusted his position and gently lifted her feet onto his lap. "Feel better?"

She nodded. "Listen, I appreciate you bringing me home and looking out for me but—"

"But nothing. I made dinner and I'm staying." He'd called Fallon and asked her to stop by his apartment and pack a few things and drop a bag off here. He knew his sister wouldn't mind and she'd been only too happy to do it. He was taking care of Samantha and he wouldn't accept an argument. "I hope you like lasagna."

Her eyes opened wide. "I love it. Did you make garlic bread?"

Laughing, he nodded.

"Who'd have thought you had talent in the kitchen?"

"Lizzie taught all of us some basic recipes so when we moved out, we wouldn't starve," he said, his tone wistful. He'd always loved Lizzie but he still wished his mother had been around to teach him.

She watched him for a few long seconds before breaking the silence. "Are you missing your mom?"

He knew they were in tune with each other but this was proof and his heart settled a bit in his chest. "I was wishing she'd been the one to teach me but not because I don't adore Lizzie. I just—"

"You miss her. It's only natural."

He rubbed his thumb back and forth over the arch

of her foot, and she moaned and his cock thickened inside his track pants.

He forced his mind onto their conversation. "I do. And I miss my biological parents, just knowing they aren't here leaves a hole in my heart. Although I know I had a more peaceful life once they were gone. Which makes for some guilt."

"I'm sorry, Dex. I despise the things my father did but I miss the idea of having a dad. Ian did his best but he was a big brother. Not my father."

"Life is complicated," he said. "Do you know where your father is?"

She sighed. "A few years ago, he had a confrontation with Savannah, his second wife, and my half-brother, Jason. He was in pretty bad financial trouble and as I mentioned, my cousins bought his hotels. But nobody hears from him." She shrugged her shoulders. "He obviously has issues. I just try and be grateful for the family I do have."

"Same." He noted the gruffness in his tone and cleared his throat. "Looks like we have more in common than we realized."

"We do."

She pushed herself up to a sitting position and he pulled her toward him and onto his lap. Her legs straddled his thighs and she faced him, a teasing smile on her face. "You know how to take my mind off of my problems."

He braced his hands on her hips and pulled her close, sealing his lips over hers. She kissed him back, threading her fingers through his hair and scraping over his scalp with her nails. The action felt good and intimate. It was so easy to feel close to her and to forget the walls she still had up.

She slowly rocked her pelvis, her sex rolling back and forth over his growing erection, and all thoughts rushed out of his head. She moaned and began gyrating faster. Gritting his teeth he pressed her into him, waiting until he felt her body stiffen and tremble, until she fell forward, her breasts pressing into his chest, her breath hot against his neck.

"We shouldn't. You need to rest."

She shook her head. "I'm fine and know what I can handle," she insisted, then pushed back and slid down until she was on her knees in front of him.

"Are you sure?"

"Shh," she said, hooking her fingers into the top of his track pants, she began to pull them down. He raised his hips and helped her ease them off, along with his boxer briefs. His cock bobbed against his stomach until she wrapped her hand around it before sliding her palm up and down his shaft.

Then, without warning, she rose up and slipped her mouth over the head of his cock, closing her lips and sliding up, releasing him with a pop.

"Fuck, that feels good."

Holding him at the base, she repeated the motion with her mouth, sucking him down until, when she looked up at him, her eyes teared and her makeup dripped down her face. But she was doing this for him and he found her beautiful.

She continued to lick and pump his erection until he was close to an orgasm, and he wanted to give her a choice. "Babe, I'm going to come."

He expected her to ease back with her mouth and pick up the rhythm with her hand, but she only sucked harder and he began to lift his hips, rising and falling, fucking into her mouth until he came so hard he saw stars. For a man with his history with women, everything with Samantha felt fresh and new.

She pushed herself to her feet and walked to the bathroom, taking time to clean up and returning with a towel for him. Once he'd taken care of things and tossed the towel in the hamper in the bathroom, they walked to the bedroom and ended up in her bed.

"You need a break," he said, as they snuggled together against the myriad of pillows she had on top of her mattress.

She sighed. "I know but I had a break in the Bahamas and I need to keep an eye on things at the office."

He had one arm behind her and pulled her tighter against him. With the other hand, he toyed with her soft hair. "From what I can tell, Brandy can handle things if you take a break."

She shook her head. "If I disappear, Jeremy will think I'm weak."

He let out a low chuckle. "The last thing anyone will think is that you're weak. Jeremy will assume you went away with your sexy boyfriend, and he'll be right."

"Away, huh? What did you have in mind?"

"Florida." He'd thought of it on the car ride home from the hospital. He just didn't know if she'd go for the idea.

"What?" She pulled away and turned to face him. "What's in Florida, other than my family? Because I don't think that's what you had in mind."

He grinned. "That's a side benefit. My house there is empty. The furniture's been put in storage up here but I need to see for myself. How about going with me? We can stay at a hotel and you can relax a bit. See your mom, whoever else is around…"

"Truth?" She treated him to a wide smile. "I would love to see my mother and family down there. But Mom's going to insist we stay at her place. She bought a new house when she remarried with rooms for everyone. If you're not comfortable, I can explain we're staying in a hotel but—"

"It's all good. We can stay wherever you want." He picked her cell up off the nightstand. "Call Brandy and your mom, arrange things, and we can leave whenever you're ready. Does tomorrow morning work for you?"

She bit down on her lower lip.

"What?" he asked.

"This might be the most spoiled thing ever but I'm going to ask Ian to send his jet."

Dex burst out laughing, but in a warm, fuzzy kind of way. She was adorable. "It is spoiled. But you should ask him anyway."

She accepted the phone and he waited while she made a bunch of calls. She spoke to Brandy, who thought it was a great idea, her mother, who couldn't wait to see her, Ian to arrange the jet, and she texted some other siblings.

"Ian wants us to have dinner with him and Riley one night," she said.

Dex forced a smile. "Oh, joy."

She burst out laughing. "Don't worry. He's much more pleasant when Riley's around."

He studied her and he relaxed, too.

"What?" she asked. "You're staring."

Shrugging, he said, "I like seeing you like this. Chill and excited."

She met his gaze and suddenly she was in his arms,

hugging him tight. "It's because of you, Dex. Thank you."

She tilted her head back and he brushed her hair from her face. "My pleasure, beautiful."

And he'd never meant words more.

# Chapter Eighteen

DEX WAS RIGHT. Going to Florida lifted a weight off Samantha's shoulders. Stepping off the plane and inhaling the humid air told her she was home. Though she loved New York, there was nothing like family.

Instead of going to Dex's house first, they rented a car and drove to her mom's house. She passed through the gates and as soon as he parked, she was out of the car and rushing up the driveway.

Her mother greeted her at the front door, wearing a pair of white Bermuda shorts, a collared shirt tied low at the waist, and her hair pulled back in a low ponytail.

"Mom!" Suddenly feeling like she wanted to cry, Samantha threw herself into her mother's arms. "It's been such a mess." Tears leaked from her eyes and though she ought to be embarrassed, letting out her frustration and pain felt cathartic. Her mother had always been there for her and now was no different.

"Shh. It's going to be okay. Let's go inside and we'll talk." She rubbed Samantha's back as she did when she was a child. "But first, aren't you going to introduce me to the good-looking man at the foot of the stairs?" she asked in a quiet voice.

"Oh right." She sniffed and dabbed at her eyes with her fingers before turning to face Dex. "Dex, this is my mom, Emma St. Claire. Mom, this is Dex Sterling. He's a friend of Ian's and he's been there for me throughout this crisis."

"I'm aware."

Dex stepped forward and shook her mother's hand. "Ms. St. Claire, it's nice to meet you."

"Same here. And thank you for being there for Samantha. I felt much better knowing she hasn't been alone. Now, let's get out of this heat and you two come inside."

Her mother's husband, Michael Brooks, walked out of the kitchen and joined them. Her mother had kept her maiden name during both marriages.

Samantha walked over and gave him a friendly hug. "Good to see you," she murmured.

"It's good to see you, too. We've both been worried and I'm glad you're here." Michael was a good man and her mother adored him. After the nightmare that was Samantha's father, her mother deserved it.

She smiled. "Thanks, but I'm okay." She left out the hospital visit. She'd save that for her mother when they were alone.

Emma introduced the men, then Michael suggested he and Dex go sit beneath the awning by the pool where they had an overhead fan. Samantha knew he was giving her time with her mom and Dex seemed at ease, so she agreed.

Following Emma into the kitchen, her mother poured them both a glass of lemonade and they settled into the barstools at the island.

"You look tired," her mother said. "You have dark circles under your eyes."

Samantha swallowed hard. "Don't panic, because you can see I'm fine, but yesterday I fainted and wound up in the hospital."

"What?! Why didn't anyone call me?" Emma asked, her voice high and frantic.

The last thing Samantha wanted was to upset her mom. "Because I'm fine. I just hadn't eaten and my blood pressure dropped. It was that and stress, which is why Dex insisted we get away."

"I like that man," her mother said.

Samantha felt her cheeks heat. "I do, too, Mom. But there was a time I liked Jeremy, too."

"Do you really think Dex is anything like your ex-fiancé?"

She immediately shook her head. "But it's so soon after the almost-wedding. Which I am so sorry for. I shouldn't have let things get that far, Mom. It cost you—"

"Stop. Better before than after the wedding, or after you've stayed so long you set a bad example for your children, or waste your younger years with the wrong man." Emma blinked back the tears in her eyes.

"Oh, Mom. You didn't set a bad example for us. If anything, you showed us strength of character. Loyalty. I admire you so much."

"And I admire *you*. You're a smart businesswoman and you think before you jump. Which is why you won't fully commit to your feelings for Dex. And that's okay. Take your time. If he's the right one, he'll wait."

"That's exactly what I needed to hear." Samantha hugged her mom tight before sitting back in her seat and taking her first sip of the tart but refreshing drink.

Her mother did the same. "Now, what do you say about me inviting the family over for an impromptu dinner? I'll order in and we'll all get together."

"I'd love that."

"Great! Then let's start making phone calls."

And just like that, she put her concerns away for the night and focused on having a good time with the family she loved.

DEX SPENT A good amount of time talking to Emma's

husband, Michael, who owned an insurance company downtown. He was a smart man and from what Dex could sense, a decent one who, though he'd only been married to Emma for a handful of years, cared about her children.

The backyard was huge, with large ceramic pots, a cactus planted in each, all surrounding the outer perimeter of the property in front of the screen that protected the pool.

They were mid-deep in conversation about this year's Thunder players when Dex's cell rang. "Excuse me," he said, pulling the phone from his pocket and taking the call from Austin.

"Hello?" Dex asked.

"Where are you?" His agent spoke without preamble.

Dex smiled at Michael before replying. "Hello to you too. And I just so happen to be in Miami."

"With Samantha."

"Yes." He had no intention of lying or hiding the fact that he cared about her and would be by her side for as long as she needed him.

Austin let out a host of expletives. "You don't listen, do you?"

Shaking his head, Dex asked, "Why should I? I'm single, she's single, this whole *it's unseemly* thing is a crock of shit and you know it."

"I do but that doesn't matter. Jeremy Rollins is doing interviews that make Samantha sound like a cheating whore and you like a home-wrecking asshole, and the reason for his called-off wedding. Peter Morgan called and wants to know why his newest analyst is getting bad press," he said of the president of FSN. How's Samantha?" he asked, changing the subject, and Dex knew it was a temporary reprieve.

"Shaky. She fainted yesterday and was in the hospital. I took her to Florida because I need to check in on my house, but mostly because I wanted her to spend time with her family."

Austin let out a long breath, followed by a curse. "You love her."

Dex glanced at Michael and pushed himself up from his chair, stepping away to take the call in private. "Is this my agent asking?"

"No. I'm asking as Samantha's cousin and your friend."

Dex stood by the screen and looked out at a lake in the distance. Wiping the sweat from his forehead with the back of his hand, he groaned, because he couldn't stay mad at this man.

"Yes, I love her." Saying the words aloud released the pressure he'd been feeling in his chest. "I love her and I am not walking away. Not when she needs me and not at all. If you want me to sit down with Morgan and ease his mind, I'll do that when I get back to New York. But she comes first."

Austin barked out a laugh. "You have never made life easy."

Dex shrugged. "That's why you're paid the big bucks. One more thing."

"What?"

Dex glanced at Michael, who was busy on his phone. Lowering his voice, he said, "I still don't want Samantha to know there's trouble with my job. She has enough on her mind." And she didn't need a reason to run from him.

"I'll do what I can to keep the people at FSN calm, but the media cycle has to focus on something else and quick."

Dex understood. "I'll tell you what. I'll try and keep things with Samantha under the radar until things blow over." It wasn't like either of them were looking to be photographed or be the focus of the paparazzi's cameras.

"Thank you," Austin said, clearly relieved.

"Talk soon and say hello to Quinn."

"Will do." He disconnected the call and Dex headed back to Michael, only to find Samantha and her mother had joined them.

Samantha's eyes were red but she seemed more relaxed and was smiling.

"Is everything okay?" she asked, as he joined them.

He nodded. "Austin was just confirming some appointments when I'm in Kansas City."

She tipped her head to one side. "Really? Because I heard raised voices."

"You know how guys joke and raise their voice."

She gave him a skeptical look but before she could ask another question, her mother spoke. "Did you tell Dex we're having a family dinner tonight?"

Samantha shook her head. "I didn't get the chance." She glanced at him. "But he knows now." Conversation turned to food and dessert. "Dex and I can pick up things at the bakery. I'm dying for one of their cannolis."

"Oh, good idea!" Emma said.

"Umm… I thought it would be smarter if you and I stayed out of the public spotlight." Dex walked over and put an arm around her waist to soften his words. "Just while things with the paparazzi blow over."

"Oh, sure. That makes sense," she said in a more subdued voice.

"I can ask Meg and Scott to pick up dessert on their way over," Emma said.

"That's my brother and his wife," Samantha explained.

"You'll have to keep everyone straight in your head," Emma said, laughing.

"I'm used to it in my big family."

Samantha smiled. "Thanks, Mom. I'm going to show Dex around and unpack our things."

Emma nodded. "Good. I'm glad you're staying over while you're here." She picked up her phone and began to text, presumably giving orders to all of Samantha's siblings.

# Chapter Nineteen

FOR THE LAST two days, Samantha and Dex had spent time with her family, sitting around the pool, bringing in lunch and dinner. When she'd suggested she and Dex sneak out for a quick dinner alone, he'd encouraged her to stay at the house. After all, she was here to see her mother and siblings. They could go out for dinner any time. Since he'd made sense, she'd agreed.

The next day, Dex drove them to the house he'd bought in Miami, located across a guard-gated bridge in an ultra-luxury community. Even for her, growing up with incredible wealth and privilege, this island was something beyond her experience.

"So," he said, as they pulled into the driveway. "You can see it's a little much."

She laughed, taking in the massive home, especially for one man living alone.

"To be honest, I bought the place after a huge contract signing, *because I could*. Only after I moved in and it echoed did I realize what a foolish move it had been."

"But it's gorgeous, Dex. Show me around inside?"

He shut the engine to the rental sports car and walked around to open her door. Together, they strode up the walkway lined with red flowering shrubs she thought were bougainvillea because they looked like the plants surrounding her childhood home.

He unlocked the door and once inside, shut off the alarm. "There isn't much to see furniture-wise since it's in storage." There were a few boxes in various rooms, waiting to be picked up and shipped, but mostly he was right. She was touring empty rooms. The place would be on the market soon, which she thought was a shame, since she'd fallen in love on sight. Maybe because the outside reminded her of her childhood home, as did the many rooms which could hold brothers and sisters like she had.

While he was inside making phone calls about the boxes and items that remained, she walked out back to look at the large, kidney-shaped pool and the built-in outdoor grill, refrigerator, and firepit. The place was lacking for nothing, she mused, and again felt a pang of sadness, this time because Dex hadn't truly loved living here and had felt so alone.

"Ready to go?" Dex asked from the sliding glass door leading out to the pool.

She nodded. "Did you get everything done that you needed to?"

"I did. The boxes will be picked up and shipped by

Monday. The company that takes care of the house will come by to open the place and facilitate things."

"That's great. What—" Her cell rang from inside her purse. "One sec," she said and dug out the phone, glancing at it. "My lawyer."

"Go ahead and take it," Dex said.

She tapped the screen and put the phone to her ear. "Hello?"

"Hi, Samantha. Tim here. I'm calling to give you an update from the forensic accountants."

She placed a supportive hand on the stone surrounding the grill. "Have they found anything off or unusual?" she asked.

She felt Dex's gaze on her as she listened.

"There are some suspicious transactions that, at a glance, make them want to dig deeper. They don't recognize the payees as having done business with your company recently and want to check further. I wanted to let you know Jeremy's lawyers have been notified, so he's likely aware, as well."

"Great," she muttered. "I appreciate the heads-up. Keep me posted."

"Will do. Take care, Samantha."

She disconnected the call. "Just what I need. Jeremy having something else to get worked up and angry over," she muttered.

Dex stepped closer. "What's wrong?"

She explained what Tim had told her and Dex immediately slipped his hand into hers. "You'll get through this."

"I know. It's just so much more than I ever expected to deal with."

He pulled her close and wrapped his arms around her. "Jeremy will be out of your life before you know it."

She breathed in deep, inhaling his masculine scent. "You smell good," she said, tilting her face to his.

He lowered his mouth, capturing her lips with a kiss that quickly turned hotter than the blazing sun above them. He lifted her and she wrapped her legs around his waist, taking advantage of their time alone. She wasn't sure how long they stood there but she was certain she'd never enjoyed kissing anyone the way she did Dex. He made it an art form, something equally important as sex in a relationship. And this was truly becoming more than friendship. Even she could admit that to herself.

By the time they came up for air, Samantha's shirt was damp from the sun and humidity and she was ready to go inside. Slipping his hand into hers, they headed in and he locked the door to the pool.

She glanced back, wishing she'd seen this place with the furniture out back, and the house filled.

"What are you thinking about?" Dex asked.

She turned to face him, smiling at the scruff that had grown on his handsome face. "This house."

He raised an eyebrow. "What about it?"

"You'll think it's silly," she said, shaking her head.

"Not a chance. Tell me."

"I can see you living here," she murmured. "Throwing a football in the yard, swimming in the pool, having barbeques out back."

"Sounds wonderful. It's a great place. Maybe for another person or family."

She tipped her head to the side and sighed. He had a point. "Yeah. You're right. Timing is everything. I hope whoever buys it is happy here." She paused, then asked, "Were you?"

He hesitated, clearly giving the question thought. "I was lonely. My family was in New York. I'd passed the point of wanting the guys over all the time, so it was a big, empty house. A status symbol."

"And you never saw it as a place to raise a family?" she finally asked.

His eyes opened wide. He obviously hadn't realized how deeply she'd been thinking. "When I lived here, I wasn't at that point in my life. And now, everything I need or want is in New York." His gaze held hers as he spoke.

Warmth settled inside her because she heard the words he wasn't saying. *She* was one of those things he both wanted and needed. And for now, that was enough.

His cell rang, breaking the intimate moment.

Dex let out a curse and stepped back, pulling his phone from his pocket and tapping the screen hard. "This had better be important," he said, walking away as he spoke.

He headed to the other side of the big space that he'd told her had once been a game room. Watching, she gnawed on the inside of her cheek, wondering why she wasn't privy to his side of the phone call. It wasn't the first time since they'd arrived in Florida. Friends called him and he spoke to them in front of her, laughing and joking. Family calls, the same.

She didn't need to be privy to all his business but this was unusual and after Jeremy's secrets, it made her uneasy.

"Everything okay?" she asked, when he strode back to her, a muscle ticking in his jaw.

"Fine. Austin just wanted to relay a message from the network. Ready to go?"

Since any warm mood had been broken, she nodded, and they headed back to her mother's house where Emma had invited both her children and Samantha's half-siblings for dinner.

Dex had gotten along well with her brothers and sisters, having come from a big family himself, and seemed totally comfortable with the large group. The girls accepted him easily and the guys gave him the third degree but once they started talking football, all possible differences disappeared.

The only thing that bothered her was the calls Dex took with Austin. He never spoke in front of her and despite wanting to ask what was wrong, she didn't want to pry.

If something was going on with his upcoming job or anything else and Dex wanted to talk about it, he would. Until then, she'd mind her own business.

# Chapter Twenty

A FEW DAYS after returning from Florida, Saman-tha stepped off the elevator to her office, her mind on Dex and their relationship. He'd been staying overnight but still holing up in her apartment and not going out for dinner so they wouldn't be seen together in public. Same as it had been in Florida, and she was getting antsy. The talk about them had died down, replaced by a pregnant, popular celebrity, but Dex had again suggested they not give Jeremy fodder for his bullshit claims that could anger him and cause him to be more difficult in the negotiations.

She'd agreed, but a big part of her hated having to hide who she was seeing when she'd done nothing wrong. But even Ian had agreed with Dex. He hadn't wanted to give Jeremy any more things to twist in his mind and lie about to the press, so he'd invited them to his home for dinner. Until she settled her business dealings with Jeremy, keeping the man level-headed was the goal. The good news was, she hadn't seen him since her return.

She headed to her office, saying hello to people as she made her way there. Her assistant sat at her usual place.

As soon as Samantha returned from Florida, Brandy had taken a few days off and this was their first time seeing each other in person.

"Hi, Brandy," Samantha said, excited to see her friend.

"Hello, and welcome home to both of us!"

She grinned. "Thanks. And thank you for holding down the fort. Again. Great job." She was aware Brandy had done double duty often since the wedding disaster.

Brandy waved off the compliment. "As long as you remember come bonus time," she said with a wink. "So... you look tan and relaxed."

"Seeing family was good for me," she admitted.

"And Dex? Was he good for you too?"

Laughing, Samantha rolled her eyes. "I'll never kiss and tell."

Brandy grinned. "As long as you kissed," she said, following Samantha into her office.

"How were your days off?" Samantha lowered herself into her chair with a sigh. It felt good to be back where she belonged.

"Lots of R and R," Brandy said. "Although I'm looking forward to my next longer vacation in the fall." Brandy had planned a trip to Jamaica and Samantha understood her excitement. "As for work," Brandy went on, "I did as you asked and kept an eye on Jeremy. He's been sneaking around, talking to the VPs and associates, schmoozing people he never bothered with before. The snake is up to something."

The peace Samantha had been feeling about work since her return disappeared. "Okay, thanks for keeping an eye out. I'll touch base with Tim," she said of her attorney. She hadn't spoken to him since the phone call in Florida.

She closed her eyes and shook her head. Was keeping this place really worth dealing with Jeremy and his bullshit? Yes, it was, dammit. At the very least she was going to walk away with what was rightfully hers.

"Good luck," Brandy murmured, her voice causing Samantha's eyes to open, and she refocused on her surroundings.

"Thanks."

Brandy walked out, shutting the door behind her.

The first thing Samantha did was leave a message for her lawyer. Then she texted Ian and asked if he'd spoken to Tim. The attorney had permission to discuss her case with her brother. Without hearing from either of the men, she dug into work.

An hour or so later, Tim called her back and asked her to come by his office. Hearing the urgency in his voice, she grabbed her purse, let Brandy know she was going to a meeting, and took a car to Midtown. She gave her name at the receptionist desk and was immediately escorted to Tim's office.

He stood as she walked in and gestured for her to take a seat in front of his desk. Once she did, he lowered himself into his chair. "Thank you for coming on such short notice."

She forced a smile, panic swirling in her stomach. "It sounded urgent."

"It is. A financial record search of your partner has uncovered a bank account in the Cayman Islands."

She blinked, certain she'd heard wrong. "I'm sorry, what?"

Tim threaded his fingers together, leaning forward as he spoke. "The forensic accountants and the investigators they hired uncovered the account. And they confirmed that the companies your firm paid, the ones that weren't a match to anyone you are doing business with, are shell corporations that funneled the money to the account in the Caymans."

Her mouth ran dry. "How much did he steal?"

The attorney shot her a sympathetic look. "Roughly five hundred thousand over a long period of time… as of now. Clearly, he planned on taking much more over time. And if he married you, he'd have been funneling whatever he could get his hands on."

She sat back in her seat, stunned. "According to our criminal litigation department, he's looking at a second degree, class C felony. That's fifteen years in prison if convicted."

Her head spun and she didn't know what to say. "What happens next?"

"We continue to dig and compile evidence. We can decide if we want to approach him with what we found or take the information to the police. Either way, you'll have decisions to make in the near future. But you should know, there's a strong likelihood Jeremy has been made aware of the search and what was discovered. He may be volatile."

She nodded. "I won't be alone with him." She'd be much more careful than prior to her Florida trip. She didn't like that she was seeing a side to her ex she'd never imagined he'd been hiding from her and the world.

When she arrived back at the office, she texted Brandy to meet her downstairs, so if she ran into Jeremy, she wouldn't be alone, and together they headed upstairs where she settled in to work.

Not long after her return, a knock sounded on the door. "Come in!" she called, shutting down the account information she'd been studying.

Leah Johnson, an associate, walked in, iPad in hand. "Sorry to bother you, but would you have time to go over the Perfect Pillow account pitch?"

Happy to think about something she enjoyed, Samantha nodded. "Come on in. Let's see what you've got."

The rest of the afternoon passed similarly, with meetings, lunch at her desk, and catch-up calls with clients. Before she knew it, it was after six p.m.

Samantha grabbed her bag and stepped out to find Brandy still at her desk. "Ready to go home?"

"Definitely. Want to grab dinner?" Brandy asked.

She nodded. "Sure."

Dex had called midday, saying he had a business meeting and if he was too late, he'd sleep at his place tonight. Once again, he'd been vague and she wasn't certain if he was pulling back or... she didn't know what. She just sometimes sensed a distance between them that hadn't been there before. It was a combination of Dex having something going on with his work that she wasn't privy to, and her protecting herself by withdrawing. So, if he walked away, she wouldn't be hurt.

Which was bullshit, she knew. If Dex broke things off, she'd be devastated. Her feelings for him had grown way beyond the friendship she purported to feel. And she had no idea what to do about it.

"Where do you want to eat?" Brandy asked.

"Why don't we go to Enzo's? I'm in the mood for pizza," Samantha suggested. Her stomach grumbled at the thought.

Brandy nodded. "I love Enzo's. Let's go."

They took the elevator downstairs and Samantha noticed they were the only two left in the office. They walked outside, turning left toward the restaurant when Samantha stopped short.

"Dammit. I think I left my phone upstairs." She opened her purse and dug around inside to be sure. "Yeah, I did. Sorry."

"I'll come back up with you," Brandy offered.

"Why don't you wait in the lobby where it's cooler? I'll go upstairs real quick and we can go to dinner." She turned and stepped toward the double doors and saw Jeremy walking outside. That was a confrontation she did not want to have and attempted to pivot in the opposite direction.

"Samantha."

She cringed at the sound of his voice but spun to face him. "What?" she asked, watching, as if in slow motion, he slid his hand inside his jacket and pulled out a gun.

"If I'm going down then so are you." He faced her and without hesitating, pulled the trigger, returned the gun to his jacket, and ran, disappearing into the rush hour crowd on the sidewalk.

She blinked, stunned. Felt the stinging burn in her upper left side, below her rib cage, and then the real pain registered, knocking the wind out of her, and she fell to her knees.

Glancing down, she saw red seeping through her dress and pressed her hand against it, coming back with sticky palms. Blood. Hers? Screaming sounded and she looked up to see it was Brandy.

A man knelt beside her and pressed his crumpled suit jacket against her and she cried out.

"Shh. I know it hurts but I have to slow the bleeding," the stranger said. "Call 911."

With shaking hands, Brandy tried to dial the numbers but kept dropping the phone.

"It's okay. I called," a woman's voice said.

Brandy crawled close to Samantha, grabbing her hand and pulling it tight against her chest, getting blood all over her dress. "You hold on. If we're lucky, it went right through and didn't hit anything."

"Watching *Grey's* again?" she asked her frightened friend, trying to make light of the situation and calm them both down. Samantha coughed, winced, and cried out.

"It's going to be okay," Brandy said, her own voice shaking. "I didn't see who did this."

"Jeremy."

Brandy gasped as Samantha coughed and cried out at the sharp pain. Sirens sounded in the distance but even Samantha knew what New York City traffic was like at this time of day and the ambulance would take a while.

"I'm cold." She began to shiver.

"She's going into shock," someone said. This time it wasn't Brandy playing doctor.

"My phone's upstairs," Samantha said to Brandy as dizziness washed over her.

The man by her side yelled for someone else to hand over their jacket. She felt him remove the bloody item covering her and replace it with another one.

"Call my bro—"

Brandy squeezed her hand. "Okay, honey. I'll call Ian. I need your code to get into the phone."

Everything swam in front of her eyes, black spots threatening to cause her to pass out. "7777."

"Oh, we're going to talk about security," Brandy muttered.

Samantha's body shook from pain. "Don't call Dex. Busy," she slurred. "Important," she forced out, as she felt herself going under and everything went black.

DEX SAT IN the second bedroom of his apartment that he used for a home office. A large monitor was in front of him, his agent's face on the screen.

"You have a business dinner with Peter Morgan in

an hour. Think you can be pleasant and not discuss the issues with paparazzi?" Austin asked.

Dex shook his head. "I won't bring it up unless he does."

"Good. Once Samantha's business issues are over, her partner will take his money and be happy, and you two are free to do whatever you want. Morgan won't care if you're dating her by that point and neither will Jeremy Rollins."

Slamming his hand on the desk, Dex leaned forward. "Do you think I give a damn what that weasel wants? I'm trying to protect Samantha. To that end, I've done what you asked. I've kept us out of sight for over a week, if you include my time in Florida."

"Good—"

"I'm not finished," Dex muttered, pissed at the world for the frustration he felt for so many reasons.

"By all means. Go on." Austin folded his arms across his chest and leaned back in his chair.

"Samantha thinks this seclusion is all about Jeremy and her business. She has no idea my career would be in jeopardy if we went out in public and Jeremy created another scene. But she's upset and tired of spending every night at home in her apartment, and I have to tell you, I'm no happier about hiding us."

Austin ran a hand over his face. "I get it. But Peter Morgan didn't hire you, his predecessor did. And

Morgan is a stickler for morality clauses."

"We did nothing wrong," Dex reminded him.

"Do you remember the two morning co-anchors who had an affair?" Austin asked. "They claimed they were already separated when they got together. It became a huge social media scandal. Next thing you know, their lawyers worked out a severance package and they were gone. And the publicity surrounding them was not pleasant."

"We can handle the publicity," Dex said. And he believed it.

"And the job? Don't you want to keep it?" Austin asked, his tone sounding like the question was rhetorical.

And maybe it should be because what normal human would turn down the money he'd been offered? But Dex had a trust fund he hadn't touched. Football money he'd saved. But he'd been hesitant to accept the opportunity to start with it because he wasn't sure he was up to the traveling.

He hadn't had a long time to decide if he'd sign with FSN. At the time, he had nothing else going on in his life, so he'd taken the position. Now, he was juggling regrets because he'd rather be in one place instead of flying from city to city for Sunday games and missing every weekend with Samantha.

"Dex! Are we having a conversation or am I talking to myself?" Austin's annoyed voice grated on him.

"I need to go." Dex had to talk to Samantha. It was enough keeping her in the dark when everything revolved around her. "I'll be in touch."

"But—"

He hit the button that disconnected them, figuring he'd deal with his agent later. He had someone more important to see.

But Dex couldn't reach Samantha by phone. Every time he dialed, the call went to voicemail. Knowing it was unlike her, he began to worry. He tried the office but Brandy had left for the day.

He was due to leave for dinner with Peter Morgan but his gut was telling him something was very wrong. He paced his apartment until the last second. After dialing her one last time, he locked up his apartment, set the alarm, and took the elevator downstairs.

A black Town Car idled outside on the street. Just as he walked to the vehicle, his cell rang. Ian Dare's name showed on the screen.

Based on gut instinct alone, his stomach turned over as he answered. "Ian."

"Samantha was shot outside her office. I can't get there for a few hours. I need to pick up my mother on the way."

The words barely registered but Dex went into strategic mode, much as he did on the field when he had an instant to figure out a play. "Which hospital?" His heart pounded hard in his chest.

Ian replied.

"I'm on my way," he said, opening the car door and sliding in. "Change of destination," he said to the driver, then gave him the hospital name before turning his attention back to the call.

# Chapter Twenty-One

ENCLOSED IN THE car, Dex sat back, bouncing his foot, frustrated already with the slow pace of the drive. "What the hell happened?" he asked Ian.

"Jeremy, that son of a bitch. Her assistant was with her and called me, she's hysterical but she was able to relay information."

He glanced at the traffic around him, noting they hit every red light, and anxiety flooded him. "Brandy called you?"

"She said it was the last thing Samantha asked of her before she passed out."

"Fuck." He slammed his hand against the seat beside him. Maybe if he hadn't been so cagey about his work and plans, trying to protect her from thinking she caused him problems, she'd have had Brandy call *him*.

"Call me as soon as you know something," Ian said. "I'll be there as soon as I can." He disconnected the call and Dex sat during rush hour, his pulse racing, as it took what felt like forever to get there.

He rushed into the hospital and a young woman was at the main desk. "I'm here for Samantha Dare.

She was brought in by ambulance."

"Are you family?" she asked.

"I'm the closest thing to family for the moment. Her mother and brother are on their way from Florida and I'm their only means of obtaining information." He pulled his phone from his pocket. "I'll call her brother and you can talk to him." With a few taps, he pulled up Ian's name from his contacts. "Look, Ian Dare. Same last name." He turned the screen toward the woman. "I can even get Samantha's mother on the phone, if that'll help."

"Okay, okay. No need. Family is fine." She scrolled through her computer and met his gaze. "Samantha Dare is currently in surgery. The waiting room is on the fifth floor. If you go there, someone will come out and ask for family members. Do yourself a favor and come up with a relationship," she said, giving him a friendly wink.

Before he could see what kind of friendly, he thanked her, accepted the sticker with VISITOR written on it, and rushed toward where a security guard pointed to the elevators.

Once in the waiting room, he called Ian who was pulling into the airport and told him what little he knew. Then he settled in for a long night.

Half an hour later, Brandy walked into the room looking dazed, a police officer by her side. She wore blue scrubs and was rubbing her hands together, obsessively. He didn't want to think about why she needed to change her clothes or wash her hands so thoroughly she was now traumatized.

"Brandy?" He spoke gently, knowing she'd been through an ordeal.

She jerked her head toward him. "Dex? What are you doing here?"

"Ian called me." Besides, Samantha was hurt. Where else would he be?

Brandy walked straight to him, burrowing her face in his chest and broke down, big gulping sobs coming from her slight frame.

"Sir? I need to talk to the victim's family. You're her…"

"Dex Sterling. Her fiancé." The word came out and he had no desire to take it back.

Brandy straightened and looked up at him. He winked at her and she seemed to understand he needed the officer to know how close he and Samantha were.

"He already questioned me." Brandy trembled.

Worried about her, Dex wrapped an arm around her. "Come on. Let's sit," he said, easing her into a chair.

Though he wanted to get the details of what happened from Brandy, who'd been with Samantha, Dex had no choice but to talk to the officer. "How can I help you?" he asked the man wearing a uniform.

"When was the last time you spoke to Ms. Dare?"

"Around lunchtime. I called to tell her I had a business dinner."

He typed in the information on a phone app and proceeded to ask him the standard questions he'd expect, mostly about her relationship with her partner. The man finally left him alone and Dex turned to Brandy and sat down beside her.

"Do you want to tell me what happened?"

She swiped the tears dripping down her face with the back of her hand. "I... We... Samantha and I walked outside. We were going to go for dinner. Then she remembered she forgot her phone upstairs, so we decided she'd go up and I'd wait in the lobby."

This was the easy part of the story, he knew, and she told it quickly, growing silent afterward. "Take your time," he said, though he wanted her to keep going.

She drew a shaky breath and continued. "Samantha turned to go inside. Someone bumped into me, so I didn't actually see what happened. It was rush hour and the sidewalk was busy."

"It's okay," he said, rubbing her back.

"I heard a loud sound. I guess the shot. Samantha turned and she was bleeding. She dropped to her

knees and I… I screamed. There was so much blood."
She shivered, her teeth chattering, and Dex shrugged
off his suit jacket so he could put it over her shoulders.

"No! No jacket."

"But you're trembling," he said, confused.

She glanced up at him. "A man used his suit jacket
to stop the bleeding. It hurt her. She cried out." She
shook her head back and forth and he laid his jacket
on the chair beside him.

"Okay, no jacket. Did Samantha say anything?" he
asked.

Rubbing her hands against her thighs, she said, "I
tried to calm her down by saying something stupid
about the bullet going straight through and she chided
me for watching *Grey's Anatomy* again. She was so cold
and shaking. But she told me to get her phone. I asked
for her code and when she gave it, I told her we really
needed to talk about security."

"You kept her talking and you were there, Brandy.
You did good."

More tears filled her eyes. "She asked me to call
her brother."

"Not me?" The words slipped from his lips.

She shook her head. "She said not to call you, then
something like you were busy, and the word important, before she passed out."

Nausea washed over him along with a pain in his

chest the likes of which he'd never felt before. "Nothing is more important than she is," he said. *Nothing.* And from this moment on, he swore she'd know it.

"I'm sorry," Brandy whispered.

"It's okay. Is there anyone I can call to sit with you?" he asked.

She shook her head. "Can I be your sidekick?"

He laughed. "Sure." He rubbed her back and together, they sat in silence.

An hour passed, then two. People came and went, waiting on loved ones. Doctors walked in, giving them news. Dex was worried sick and losing his mind, but he knew making a scene at the nearby desk wouldn't help. When they had news, someone would come find them.

Brandy had huddled in a more comfortable chair in the corner but after a while, he couldn't sit still. Rising to his feet, he paced the room, checking his watch nonstop. At this point it was a toss-up who he'd see first, Ian or the surgeon. He ultimately grew tired and sat back down, his head in his hands.

"The family of Samantha Dare?" A doctor stood in the entrance and Dex rose to his feet. Brandy followed.

And as if he'd had a line to the operating room, Ian, his wife, Riley, and Emma joined them, rushing in and around the man to hear what he had to say.

"I'm her mother," Emma said, and Ian put an arm around her shoulders. Pale and shaking, Samantha's mother waited for news.

"She made it through surgery." He said the words and a collective breath and sigh of relief echoed around the room.

Dex felt as though he could breathe for the first time since getting Ian's call.

"Oh, thank God." Emma clasped her hands in front of her chest.

"What else?" Ian asked, in his no-nonsense voice.

The doctor nodded. "The bullet nicked her spleen."

Riley gasped and Emma grabbed her hand.

"We were able to repair the damage and retrieve the bullet. She's a lucky woman and barring any complications, she should heal and be okay."

"Oh, thank God," Brandy said, and Dex pulled her against him. She'd been through so much tonight. They all had. Dex had almost lost his better half and it was time he let her know how he felt.

"When can we see her?" Ian asked.

The older man cleared his throat. "She's in recovery. Once she's settled, we'll let you see her, one person at a time."

Everyone let out another sigh of relief.

Dex was so fucking relieved she'd be okay, he sat

down and dipped his head, letting himself breathe.

Ian tilted his head, indicating he wanted to talk, and they stepped to a private corner of the room. "Why the fuck would Jeremy shoot her?"

Brandy, who'd been standing since the doctor left, walked over. "I heard you talking. Samantha had a meeting with her lawyer this morning. We were going to talk over dinner. She didn't want to discuss it at the office, but I think he might know more?"

Ian nodded. "Thanks. I'll go leave him an urgent message."

"Thanks, Brandy. Are you okay? Can I get you something to eat or drink?" Dex offered.

She shook her head. "I think since you're all here and going to want to see her, I'll go home. Will you keep in touch?"

Dex touched her shoulder. "Of course. I'll walk you out and wait with you until the car comes. You've had a rough evening. You don't need to stand outside alone."

She treated him to a smile. "Thanks, Dex. I appreciate it."

"Let's go." Dex stopped by where Ian, Riley, and Emma were sitting. "I'll be back after I get Brandy safely into a car. Did you reach the attorney?" he asked Samantha's brother.

Ian shook his head. "Left a message."

Dex let out a long breath. Now that they knew Samantha would be okay, he wanted to know what the hell had tipped Jeremy into insanity, where the son of a bitch had disappeared to, and when the cops would find him.

"But the minute I find out, I want a conversation with that bastard," Ian said, his face turning red with anger.

Riley put a hand on his forearm. "Calm down. Today's been stressful enough. I don't need you having a heart attack on me."

"I'm young and healthy," he told her and she merely rolled her eyes.

Dex laughed, appreciating the lightness breaking up the painful mood of earlier. He glanced at Ian, his lips firming before he spoke, much more serious this time. "Once you have answers, I want in on that conversation with Jeremy," Dex said and Ian nodded without an argument.

Progress with Samantha's brother and his old friend, Dex assumed. Not that he thought the police would let them anywhere near Jeremy once they found him, but it was worth trying.

He escorted Brandy to her car downstairs, then joined the family as they all settled in to wait for permission to see Samantha.

# Chapter Twenty-Two

SAMANTHA'S ENTIRE BODY hurt. She came in and out of consciousness, the pain drawing her back under, an escape she was eager to give in to.

She woke to her mother's voice, which seemed odd. Her mom was in Florida. The next time consciousness came, she heard Ian, too, but he hadn't mentioned flying up anytime soon. Just as the thought occurred, she sunk back into the darkness calling her.

She wasn't certain how much time had passed when she opened her eyes and felt more clearheaded. She blinked into the lights above her. A nurse was there to check her vitals and give her ice chips, and she fell back to sleep.

The next time she woke up, she was in her own hospital room and she felt a heavy weight at her side. She glanced down to see Dex had fallen asleep, his head on the mattress beside her.

She threaded her fingers through his hair and let her nails lightly scrape along his scalp. All the while, she searched her memory for what had brought her here. Her head hurt, not to mention her left side throbbed with pain.

She remembered being outside with Brandy, going back for her phone and… "Jeremy!" she exclaimed. "He shot me."

"You're awake. Thank God," Dex said, relief in his tone, as he raised his head and her hand fell to her side. "You scared the hell out of me." His eyes were bloodshot and a scruff of beard was on his face, telling her he'd been here all night.

She realized now her family probably had flown to New York and hearing their voices hadn't been a dream. But it was Dex who stayed the night, his head beside her on the bed, and her heart swelled with emotion, her throat thick.

"You've been in and out of consciousness and I'm so relieved you're awake." His gaze took her in, his eyes softening.

"Must be the good drugs they're giving me," she said with a small smile, as she lifted her arm with the IV and needle in her hand. "I can't imagine how much worse the pain would be without them." Her eyelids were heavy but she forced herself to stay awake. "Am I okay?"

He clasped her hand and lifted it to his cheek. "You're very okay. You got lucky. A small nick to your spleen that the doctor repaired *and* they retrieved the bullet, which should help when they find Jeremy." His voice took in a deep, angry tone at her ex's name. "Do you have any idea why he lost his mind and shot you?"

She nodded. "I think so. I met with Tim yesterday, my lawyer. The forensic accountants discovered Jeremy has been embezzling from the business for a long period of time." She slid her tongue over her dry lips and Dex reached over to give her a cup filled with ice chips.

She tipped some into her mouth and sighed in relief.

"Good?" Dex asked.

She nodded and handed back the cup.

"So that bastard was stealing from you?" he asked, clenching his jaw in fury.

She nodded, then struggled to remember the details her lawyer had given her. "Those payments the accountants found had gone to shell corporations, and the money was then sent to an offshore account Jeremy opened in the Caymans."

"That son of a bitch." Dex met her gaze but did not release his tight grip on her hand, holding on as if she might disappear if he let go.

She couldn't imagine what he'd been through last night, knowing if the situation had been reversed and he'd been shot, she would have been frantic.

*Because she loved him.*

The thought hit like a thunderbolt despite the feelings having been there all along. She'd been pushing them away, telling herself they were wrong since she'd recently been about to marry another man. Attempting to convince herself she needed to figure out her life. What a fool she'd been. Without Dex in it, she didn't have a life, not the one she wanted, anyway.

"Are you okay?" he asked.

Her gaze fell to his as she took in his haggard face, no less handsome for being so exhausted. The desire to reach out and stroke his cheek was strong but she waited, needing to get through the discussion about Jeremy before she turned the subject to them.

"I am. It's just unbelievable to think back over what happened yesterday," she said, which was true.

He inclined his head. "If you're up to telling me, what happened next?"

She gestured for more ice chips and he helped her take some and wet her mouth before answering. "Tim warned me Jeremy had probably been alerted to the forensic search and results they'd found, and that he might be volatile."

"That's an understatement," Dex ground out.

"Yes. But I told him I'd be careful." Thinking back, she realized how unsuspecting she'd been, never considering how badly things could turn.

"Why didn't you call me?" he asked gruffly. She sensed the hurt behind the words but there'd been no real reason to think she needed him at that point in time.

"I thought I could handle Jeremy." She gave Dex a little shrug, her cheeks warming with embarrassment. "Based on his recent behavior with me, I figured not being alone would keep him from approaching me again. I never thought he'd *shoot* me. I didn't know he even owned a gun." She shivered at the reminder of the moment the bullet struck and the pain afterward.

She squeezed Dex's hand, fear taking hold. "He can't get in here, right? I mean, I'm safe?"

He shook his head and gently caressed his fingers along her cheek, causing her to tremble even more. "You're fine. I'm not leaving and your brother has a security guard outside. A female who is as unobtrusive as she can be. Ian moves quickly."

She managed a smile at his accurate description of her brother.

As for Dex not leaving… "You need to eat, shower, and sleep," she said gently. "And I'm relieved there's a guard." She let out a long breath, feeling better about being stuck here.

She lay her head back on the pillow. No sooner had she done so than her thoughts went back over the hours prior to the shooting. And the days after they'd returned from Florida. Things had been hot and cold between them and she had only herself to blame.

"Dex—"

"Samantha—"

She laughed at their mind-meld.

"Ladies first," he said. She noted her hand was still in his, his fingers wrapped protectively around hers.

"Okay." She paused for a moment, gathering her thoughts. "I don't know if this is the right time but we need to talk."

He slid his chair in closer, a concerned look on his face. "Go on."

"Before I got shot, you said you had a business dinner and might not come by. Now, don't get me wrong, we aren't living together. You don't owe me every night. But—" She picked at the blanket tucked around her with her free hand, not meeting his gaze. "Things between us have been weird. Off."

"I know and I can explain," he said.

Now she did look at him and saw regret in his sad eyes and expression. "Can I say one more thing first?" she asked.

"Of course." He brushed her hair off her cheek and tucked it behind her ear. "I'm listening."

She swallowed hard, the words not coming out easily. Nerves settled in her belly and her stomach pitched, but it was time to lay out for him what she just realized herself.

She was certain about loving him and she knew what she wanted. Whether she'd driven him so out of his mind with confusing messages, he felt differently, she'd find out. Though his behavior now gave her the courage to admit her feelings.

"I realize that I was giving you mixed signals."

"Sweetheart, no—"

"I was," she insisted. "I said I wasn't looking for a relationship, that we're friends, but you were there. Every time I needed you, you stepped up without asking. And if I regret one thing, it's not giving you all of me the same way. But I noticed the change in you after Florida, and I just need to know if it's us you aren't sure of." She swallowed past her dry mouth. "Or if you think you were doing what I wanted, giving me space? Or if my issues are just too much?"

He held up a hand. "Samantha, stop. Please." He visibly shuddered, his emotions clearly on the surface, too. "I screwed up, not you. I understood why you needed time to cement your feelings. But when those photos of us came out, Austin called and said the president of the network was furious about the bad publicity. That I didn't want to give him a reason to pull the deal based on the morality clause in my contract."

She gasped. "Oh my God." She pulled her hand out of his and covered her mouth for a brief moment. "Why didn't you tell me? I knew Austin was worried but I didn't know how serious things were. I never would have gone to Florida with you or—"

"Which is exactly why I didn't tell you. I knew you'd pull away, and that was the last thing I wanted." He ran a hand through his hair, his stress obvious. "I want you, Samantha. Not an announcer spot that comes with qualifications. I kept us hidden so Jeremy didn't get upset enough to do something crazy. Which he obviously did anyway. Not to protect some job."

Discovering all he'd been keeping to himself, hearing that to him, she came first, tears formed in her eyes and she blinked in a futile attempt to hold them back. "Oh, Dex. I messed things up so badly."

"You didn't. I did." He brushed away the moisture on her cheek with his thumb. "You were shot and I was nowhere to be found. All my attempts to protect you from Jeremy by not giving him anything to worry about accomplished nothing but make you think you couldn't turn to me. You called Ian." His jaw worked back and forth in frustration.

"Because Jeremy is obviously mentally unstable and I completely missed the signs before the wedding, so how could I expect you to see them?" she asked, falling back on logic.

His deep groan echoed what she felt inside but she was finished talking about Jeremy.

"Dex?" Reaching out, she put her hand over his and squeezed, more for her own benefit than his because she needed his strength for what she was about to say. "I should have called you and not Ian… because I love you. I should have accepted that truth sooner and not let anything come between us."

His beautiful blue eyes opened wide in surprise. "You love me?"

She nodded and his sexy lips turned up as the truth settled in.

He reached out and wrapped a gentle hand around her neck and leaned forward so she didn't have to. "That's good because I love you too, Samantha Dare."

She let out a long breath, every muscle in her body easing in relief that she hadn't driven him away. "I'm so glad." She blinked and this time happy tears dripped down her cheeks.

He swiped them away and touched his lips to hers, kissing her softly, before pulling back. "You need to rest but I'm not going anywhere."

With a grateful smile, she closed her eyes. She might be in the hospital and in pain. Jeremy might still be out there, running from the police. And she had many loose ends to tie up business-wise. But as far as her personal life was concerned, she had the man she loved and that made her blissfully happy.

"I love you, Dex. And you're not giving up a job most men would kill for. Not for me."

He let out a low chuckle. "I'll make the choice

that's best for me. For us." He curled his hand around hers and though she felt his eyes on her, she drifted into a medication-induced sleep.

ONCE SAMANTHA FELL into a deep sleep, Dex stepped out of her hospital room to make a few phone calls, including smoothing things over with the head of FSN. But first he leaned against the wall and let out a groan filled with relief. From the moment Ian called him to say Samantha had been shot, Dex felt like he'd stopped breathing.

He and her family had taken turns going in to sit with her last night, Ian having pulled strings the billionaire seemed to have in every state. Dex had finally convinced Ian to take his mom to the hotel to get some rest and promised he wouldn't leave Samantha. Despite the doctor telling them she would recover, until she'd woken up and begun talking to him, he hadn't taken a full breath. Or so he thought.

Until she said those three words. Words he'd planned on saying first. Not that he cared about the order of things as long as Samantha was finally his.

He wished the situation with Jeremy was under control and the man behind bars. But his former NYPD detective brother, Remy, promised he'd pull in his favors and look into the search for the man who'd shot Samantha.

Heart pounding, he pulled out his phone and checked messages. He'd let his family know where he was but he'd been so focused on Samantha, he'd forgotten to check in. And they were not happy.

He nodded at the security guard and she stepped closer to the entrance to Samantha's room. Feeling better, he walked to an area where he could make phone calls and not disturb other patients and their families, and set about reassuring his siblings and dad.

NOT LONG AFTER their intimate discussion, an NYPD detective arrived to interview Samantha about the shooting. Dex sat by her side, holding her hand in his, as she recounted the entire situation with Jeremy. Dex's presence gave her strength but by the time she ended the story of Jeremy shooting her, she was exhausted. Throughout the telling, Dex had remained silent and didn't interrupt the questioning until her voice began to slur.

So soon after surgery, the detective was overly persistent, something she understood but she was wiped out. Only after Dex threatened to call the nurses in to ask the man to leave, did he consent to go, but said he'd be back to follow up in case she remembered anything new.

True to his word, he'd returned around dinnertime but didn't stay long. Nor did he provide them with any information about Jeremy or whether they knew his whereabouts.

The next visitor was Brandy, and Dex took a break so they could be alone.

Having shared such a traumatic event, they cried on each other's shoulders. "You saved my life, you know," Samantha said.

Brandy shook her head. "I screamed, my hand shook too hard to dial 911…"

"But you held my hand and talked me through the pain. I couldn't have made it without you there by my side," Samantha said over the lump in her throat.

"You were cracking *Grey's Anatomy* jokes," her best friend said, blinking back tears.

Samantha laughed. "Someone had to keep you calm."

Brandy wiped her eyes and smiled. "I'm so glad you're okay. I don't think I've ever been so frightened in my life."

"Same," she whispered, the memories way too close for her liking. "So… how would you like a raise?" she asked, switching topics.

Brandy's eyes opened wide. "I already know you

need me to run things at the office. Don't insult your best friend by offering me more money to help you out."

"Sit down. Please."

Pulling up a chair, Brandy lowered herself into it. "I'll be there for whatever you need."

It was Samantha's turn for tears. "Thank you. But we will revisit this raise thing soon."

She nodded. They spent the rest of her visit on lighter subjects and Brandy left when Dex returned.

TWO MORE DAYS passed, in which Dex only left Samantha's side to do as she'd said, shower, eat something, and catch some sleep. The same with her family.

Finally, the surgeon walked in on day four for his morning visit. The family stepped out so he could examine the surgical site and he called them back in to give her the good news. If she maintained her progress, the doctor said he'd discharge her the following morning. Dex knew exactly where she'd be going, too, and it wasn't back to the apartment with the memories of the man who'd hurt her both emotionally and physically.

After the surgeon walked out of the room, her

mother jumped up from her chair. "I'm so relieved!" Emma said, hugging her daughter.

Samantha, happy but still pale, smiled. "You should go home to Michael, and you two to your kids," she said to her family.

Emma shook her head. "You need me right now. Michael would have come but, like I told you, he'd just gotten over the flu and didn't want to pass anything on."

"I know, Mom. He's a good man. I'm so happy for you." She reached out and squeezed her mom's hand.

The similar warm dynamic between this family and Dex's own wasn't lost on him.

Ian strode over to his mother and put an arm around her waist. "Something tells me Samantha is in good hands and we can go home soon."

He glanced at Dex with a surprising approving look, his gaze friendlier than any time since Dex had whisked his sister off to the Bahamas. Or was it vice versa?

"Is that your approval I'm finally getting?" Dex asked.

"Speaking of your approval, Ian, we don't need it. We didn't need it all those years ago, either," Samantha said in a chiding voice.

"What's going on?" Emma asked, looking between her two children.

Riley put an arm on her mother-in-law's shoulder. "Ian was being Ian. Come outside and I'll explain."

Arm in arm, the women strode out the door.

Dex glanced at Samantha, who attempted to cross her arms over her chest, then realized the pain was too much and winced.

"Watch it, sweetheart," Dex said, hating to see her in any more pain than necessary with recovery. "You can glare at Ian all you want but no sudden movements."

Ian raised a cocky eyebrow. "Seriously? You two think if you'd gotten together when she was young and you were so involved in football it would have lasted? I did you a favor." His voice was as smug as his expression. "Besides, second chance romances are hot these days. Or so Riley says from reading romance novels," he muttered, his cheeks flushing in embarrassment over what he'd just said.

Samantha laughed as did Dex.

"I gotta tell you, that was worth its weight in gold," Dex told his friend. Because despite the banter and warnings, they were friends.

Soon to be family, if Dex had his way.

"Ian, you know I love you, right? And I turn to you when I need help. But you've got to let me live my life," Samantha said.

Her brother let out a grumbling noise. "I'm still

keeping an eye on him." He pointed to Dex.

She opened her mouth to argue but he interrupted. "Sounds fair since I'd do the same with my sister." He winked at Samantha, who despite being weak, worn out, and recovering, was still beautiful to him. "He's given us his approval, sweetheart. Take it as a win."

"Not that we need it," they said at the same time and burst out laughing.

Ian rolled his eyes. "You're lucky I love you, Sammy Bean. I'm going to find my wife."

"Sammy Bean?" Dex turned to the woman he loved and who he'd all but decided had one nickname.

*Beautiful.* That's what he called her and how he thought of her.

*Mine*, came next.

Her cheeks were bright red. "Come over here and kiss me," she said, clearly wanting to change the subject.

Good thing he was on board.

# Chapter Twenty-Three

S AMANTHA HAD BEEN home for three days… at Dex's home, she amended. He'd been insistent she come to his apartment so he could take care of her in a place where she had no memories of Jeremy. Put like that, how could she refuse? She had no desire to return to the unit she'd shared with her ex. And she wanted to be with Dex.

She lay beneath a blanket on the sofa in the living room, frustrated by her inability to move without pain. She still needed to take the narcotics they'd sent her home with from the hospital and warned her she might need them for a short while. Not to overdo it. She was grateful to have Dex taking care of her but over being immobile and in pain when she moved.

After she'd settled in with Dex, her mother, Ian, and Riley had gone home but not until they'd brought over a suitcase of her comfiest clothes, and courtesy of the women, her toiletries. The rest of her siblings had been FaceTiming her nonstop and with so many of them, she'd had to limit how long she could talk to each between naps. Even Dex's siblings, his father, and girlfriend, Lizzie, had stopped by for short visits, which she appreciated, as it gave her time to get to know them better.

The doorbell rang and she remained where she was.

"I've got it," Dex called out and walked out from the office where he'd been on a long business call. They hadn't discussed his situation with the network since their last conversation and she didn't know what he planned to do, but he'd been tied up on the phone for a while.

He strode to the entry and she heard the sound of mumbled male voices before Dex finally returned with Remy and the NYC detective who'd interviewed her.

"Are you up to talking?" Dex asked.

She nodded and carefully shifted to a more upright position, working with the discomfort. "Yes. What can I do for you, Detective?"

"I'm glad to see you've been released from the hospital. May I sit?"

She nodded, noting that Dex had settled in by her stretched-out feet, and Remy stood by his side.

The detective cleared his throat and leaned forward. "We started by checking the CCTV cameras outside your building during the shooting. Jeremy ducked into the nearest subway station, which necessitated watching footage of each stop to see if he exited somewhere with a *working* camera."

He said the last word with disgust, indicating his frustration with technology. She knew from watching the news about the lack of funding to pay for repairs and updated videos cams, and didn't blame him for his reaction.

"Any luck?" she asked, though she already sensed the answer.

He shook his head. "No. We'd also been working the family angle, interviewing those close to Jeremy Rollins. Mother, father, sister, friends, and his ex-girlfriend."

"Marley?" Samantha had no idea whether or not those two were still together. She hadn't given it any thought.

"Yes. Marley Simmons."

She made a face of distaste the detective ignored.

"His family closed ranks," he went on.

No surprise there, Samantha thought.

"But Marley was happy to cooperate—after being reminded she was Mr. Rollins's personal assistant since the business opened... and until recently, there was every likelihood we could make a case against her as an accessory."

Shocked, Samantha sat forward and immediately regretted the motion, moaning. "Ouch. Dammit."

Dex squeezed her foot. "Careful," he said in a concerned voice.

Marley being involved was something she'd never considered, but she hadn't had much time to think between discovering her ex had been embezzling and the shooting.

"Can you make a case against Marley?" Samantha asked.

"We are investigating every angle," the detective said, sidestepping the question and being cagey with his answer. "But she did mention a cabin Rollins purchased that never came up during our questioning of the family or records search. Apparently, the two of them spent time together there," he said, shooting Samantha an apologetic glance.

She shook her head, well past caring about what Jeremy had done to her. If she was going to be all in with Dex, her romantic past no longer mattered.

"Go on," she said, wanting the story not the sordid details.

The men glanced at each other, the detective nodding at Dex. Obviously this was what they'd talked about before joining her in the living room. Nerves fluttered in her stomach as she wondered what had them so on edge.

"Samantha, when they approached the cabin..." Dex cleared his throat, stalling, clearly reluctant to finish.

She sent him an imploring look, her eyes on his.

"Tell me."

"Jeremy killed himself," he said, his voice soft.

She gasped. "He *what?*"

Dex gently lifted her feet and maneuvered her so he was closer, offering comfort. "Apparently, the prospect of prison for embezzlement and attempted murder was too much for him. That, or he was filled with regret and remorse."

"But we'll never know," the detective said.

"No note?" she asked, wondering how Jeremy had reached this awful point and aware it would always be a big question. She rubbed the pain in her chest that wouldn't be leaving her for a long while.

"No," Remy said, speaking up for the first time. He'd obviously come for moral support and she was grateful for the strength she got from her family, as well as Dex's.

She lifted her hand to her cheeks, realized she had tears in her eyes and didn't understand why. After all he'd done to her… but they'd had a past. Had plans. Shared good times until things had changed.

"I think that's enough for today," Dex spoke for her and she was grateful.

"Come on," Remy said to the detective. "Let's go. I'll check in on you later, honey," he said to Samantha.

She swallowed hard. "Thank you. Really."

"If we have more questions to tie up loose ends?"

the detective asked her.

"You know where to find me," she told him.

The two men walked out and as soon as they were gone, Dex gently lifted her and settled her on his lap. "Okay?" he asked. "No pain?"

"No pain. Not when you're holding me," she said, placing her head on his shoulder.

Unable to stop the tears, she let them flow. "I'm sorry. I'm just sad for the man he was before he let greed destroy him."

He rubbed her back. "Don't apologize for having feelings about this. I'd be more worried if you didn't. You were with Jeremy for a while and this… It's a lot to process."

She nodded into his neck, inhaling his familiar scent and taking comfort from his warmth and caring. "I'm so glad I have you."

"Back at you, beautiful. We'll get through this together."

# Epilogue

*Two Months Later*

SAMANTHA SAT IN the front passenger seat of Dex's G Wagon as he drove her... somewhere. She felt for the silk tie around her eyes and her stomach flipped with excitement.

"Where are we going?" she asked for the umpteenth time, though she knew he wouldn't give her an answer. Everything inside her tingled at the prospect of the unknown.

She heard the click of the signal and felt the car make a right turn.

"If I wanted you to know, you wouldn't be blindfolded," he said, his voice sounding deeper when it was all she could focus on.

The car came to a stop and she heard him put the vehicle in park. It was amazing the noises she recognized without sight.

"Sit tight. I'll come get you," he said, and opened his car door.

He opened hers and helped her out, guiding her with his arm around her waist, but remaining silent. Building anticipation.

She thought they took an elevator a short way up but she was still lost to her whereabouts.

"Stop," he said, then she heard him opening a door. "And walk again." He led her outside… yes, definitely outside, as she felt the slightly cooler air surrounding her.

He turned her body to face whatever direction he wanted her, then let go. "Okay, now you can take the blindfold off."

She removed the silk tie covering her eyes to see they were at the outdoor movie theater they'd gone to on their first real date. On the screen were the words *MARRY ME* and in front of her, Dex had lowered himself to one knee.

She gasped, surprise filling her. True, they'd moved in together, and they'd discussed a future, but he'd kept this plan close to his chest. "Dex!"

He opened a small jeweler's box. Inside was a ring with a traditional round diamond surrounded by smaller stones creating a flowered look, but the center diamond itself was huge.

"Surprise," he said, a smile on his face.

"I had no idea," she said, her heart in her throat.

He winked, treating her to that sexy grin she adored. "Now for my speech."

She held his gaze, so in love she was filled to the brim with it.

Drawing a deep breath, he began. "From the moment I met you, I knew you were the one. I'm just so damned glad fate gave me another shot. I promise to give you all of me and never bail when things are tough. We've already had our ups and downs and we know we can face anything together. I love you, Samantha. Will you marry me?"

"Yes!" she squealed as he slid the ring on her finger. Tears of happiness filled her eyes and she suddenly realized they were surrounded by applause… and both of their large families. Her entire crew had flown up from Florida to be there for this special moment.

Dex stood, pulled her into his arms, and swept her into a long, inappropriate-for-company kiss. And neither one of them cared.

They spent the rest of the evening celebrating with their parents, siblings and their spouses, all of them enjoying champagne and hot food Dex had had catered because he'd taken over the entire theater floor. Again. There was also a DJ who arrived to play after the cocktails and though Dex still chose not to dance, he did save her the slow ones. And when he pulled her against him, he took full advantage, his hard body cradling hers as they swayed back and forth.

Ever since she'd healed from the bullet and surgery, life with Dex had been a dream. After the news broke about her shooting and Jeremy, she'd gone through a rough period of ups and downs. She'd been sad for what he'd done, upset for his family, and selfishly worried about Dex and what more negative publicity would mean for his job.

It turned out, she hadn't needed to be concerned. He'd been ready with an answer. All those conversations he'd had locked in his office had been with Austin and the network head. Dex had wanted out of his contract. He said he had no desire to be in a job that took him away every weekend. And with his dad's health questionable, he'd wanted to be close to home.

Peter Morgan had been amenable to working out a different deal with Dex. The network head had his own choice for the analyst job on Sunday nights. So Dex Sterling was now a morning co-anchor on a major sports network, replacing the longtime favorite anchor who'd retired.

Life was perfect and after so much drama and pain, she was grateful for the change.

"Where did your mind go?" Dex asked, breaking her out of her musings as he continued to sway with her.

She looked up into his sky blue eyes. "I was thinking about how I'm going to have the most perfect life because I have you. And in return, I promise to give you all of me and an equally amazing life."

Smiling, he lowered his head and sealed their promises with a long kiss.

Thanks for reading!

**Want even more Carly books?**

CARLY'S BOOKLIST by Series – visit:
https://www.carlyphillips.com/CPBooklist

Sign up for Carly's Newsletter:
https://www.carlyphillips.com/CPNewsletter

Join Carly's Corner on Facebook:
https://www.carlyphillips.com/CarlysCorner

Carly on Facebook:
https://www.carlyphillips.com/CPFanpage

Carly on Instagram:
https://www.carlyphillips.com/CPInstagram

# Carly's Booklist

*The Kingstons — newest series first*

## The Sterling Family

Book 1: Just One More Moment (Remington Sterling & Raven Walsh)

Book 2: Just One More Dare (Dex Kingston & Samantha Dare)

Book 3: Just One More Temptation (Noah Powers & Fallon Sterling)

## The Kingston Family

Book 1: Just One Night (Linc Kingston & Jordan Greene)

Book 2: Just One Scandal (Chloe Kingston & Beck Daniels)

Book 3: Just One Chance (Xander Kingston & Sasha Keaton)

Book 4: Just One Spark (Dash Kingston & Cassidy Forrester)

Book 5: Just One Wish (Axel Forrester)

Book 6: Just One Dare (Aurora Kingston & Nick Dare)

Book 7: Just One Kiss (Knox Sinclair & Jade Dare)

Book 8: Just One Taste (Asher Dare & Nicolette Bettencourt)

Novella: Just Another Spark (Dash Kingston & Cassidy Forrester)

Book 9: Just One Fling (Harrison Dare & Winter Capwell)

Book 10: Just One Tease (Zach Dare & Hadley Stevens)

Book 10.5: Just One Summer (Maddox James & Gabriella Davenport)

## *The Dares — newest series first*

### Dare Nation

Book 1: Dare to Resist (Austin & Quinn)

Book 2: Dare to Tempt (Damon & Evie)

Book 3: Dare to Play (Jaxon & Macy)

Book 4: Dare to Stay (Brandon & Willow)

Novella: Dare to Tease (Hudson & Brianne)

*\* Paul Dare's sperm donor kids*

### The Sexy Series

Book 1: More Than Sexy (Jason Dare & Faith)

Book 2: Twice As Sexy (Tanner & Scarlett)

Book 3: Better Than Sexy (Landon & Vivienne)

Novella: Sexy Love (Shane & Amber)

### The Knight Brothers

Book 1: Take Me Again (Sebastian & Ashley)

Book 2: Take Me Down (Parker & Emily)

Book 3: Dare Me Tonight (Ethan Knight & Sienna Dare)

Novella: Take The Bride (Sierra & Ryder)

Take Me Now – Short Story (Harper & Matt)

**NY Dares Series (NY Dare Cousins)**

Book 1: Dare to Surrender (Gabe & Isabelle)

Book 2: Dare to Submit (Decklan & Amanda)

Book 3: Dare to Seduce (Max & Lucy)

**Dare to Love Series**

Book 1: Dare to Love (Ian & Riley)

Book 2: Dare to Desire (Alex & Madison)

Book 3: Dare to Touch (Dylan & Olivia)

Book 4: Dare to Hold (Scott & Meg)

Book 5: Dare to Rock (Avery & Grey)

Book 6: Dare to Take (Tyler & Ella)

A Very Dare Christmas – Short Story (Ian & Riley)

*\* Sienna Dare gets together with Ethan Knight in **The Knight Brothers** (Dare Me Tonight).*

*\* Jason Dare gets together with Faith in the **Sexy Series** (More Than Sexy).*

For the most recent Carly books, visit CARLY'S BOOKLIST page

www.carlyphillips.com/CPBooklist

*Other Indie Series — newest series first*

## Hot Heroes Series
Book 1: Touch You Now (Kane & Halley)
Book 2: Hold You Now (Jake & Phoebe)
Book 3: Need You Now (Braden & Juliette)
Book 4: Want You Now (Kyle & Andi)

## Bodyguard Bad Boys
Book 1: Rock Me (Ben & Summer)
Book 2: Tempt Me (Austin & Mia)
Novella: His To Protect (Shane & Talia)

## Billionaire Bad Boys
Book 1: Going Down Easy (Kaden & Lexie)
Book 2: Going Down Fast (Lucas & Maxie)
Book 3: Going Down Hard (Derek & Cassie)
Book 4: Going In Deep (Julian & Kendall)
Going Down Again – Short Story (Kaden & Lexie)

For the most recent Carly books, visit CARLY'S
BOOKLIST page
www.carlyphillips.com/CPBooklist

## Carly's Originally Traditionally Published Books

**Serendipity's Finest Series**
Book 1: Perfect Fit (Mike & Cara)
Book 2: Perfect Fling (Cole & Erin)
Book 3: Perfect Together (Sam & Nicole)
Book 4: Perfect Strangers (Luke & Alexa)

**Serendipity Series**
Book 1: Serendipity (Ethan & Faith)
Book 2: Kismet (Trevor & Lissa)
Book 3: Destiny (Nash & Kelly)
Book 4: Fated (Nick & Kate)
Book 5: Karma (Dare & Liza)

**Costas Sisters**
Book 1: Under the Boardwalk (Quinn & Ariana)
Book 2: Summer of Love (Ryan & Zoe)

**Ty and Hunter**
Book 1: Cross My Heart (Ty & Lilly)
Book 2: Sealed with a Kiss (Hunter & Molly)

**The Lucky Series**
Book 1: Lucky Charm (Derek & Gabrielle)
Book 2: Lucky Streak (Mike & Amber)
Book 3: Lucky Break (Jason & Lauren)

**The Most Eligible Bachelor Series**
Book 1: Kiss Me if You Can (Sam & Lexie)
Book 2: Love Me If You Dare (Rafe & Sara)

## The Hot Zone

Book 1: Hot Stuff (Brandon & Annabelle)

Book 2: Hot Number (Damian & Micki)

Book 3: Hot Item (Riley & Sophie)

Book 4: Hot Property (John & Amy)

## The Chandler Brothers

Book 1: The Bachelor (Roman & Charlotte)

Book 2: The Playboy (Rick & Kendall)

Book 3: The Heartbreaker (Chase & Sloane)

## The Simply Series

Book 1: Simply Sinful (Kane & Kayla)

Book 2: Simply Scandalous (Logan & Catherine)

Book 3: Simply Sensual (Ben & Gracie)

Book 4: Body Heat (Jake & Brianne)

Book 5: Simply Sexy (Colin & Rina)

## Carly Classics

Book 1: The Right Choice (Mike & Carly)

Book 2: Perfect Partners (Griffin & Chelsie)

Book 3: Unexpected Chances (Dylan & Holly)

Book 4: Worthy of Love (Kevin & Nikki)

For the most recent Carly books, visit CARLY'S
BOOKLIST page

www.carlyphillips.com/CPBooklist

## *Carly's Still Traditionally Published Books*

**Stand-Alone Books**

Brazen

Secret Fantasy

Seduce Me

The Seduction

More Than Words Volume 7 – Compassion Can't Wait

Naughty Under the Mistletoe

Grey's Anatomy 101 Essay

For the most recent Carly books, visit CARLY'S BOOKLIST page

www.carlyphillips.com/CPBooklist

# About the Author

NY Times, Wall Street Journal, and USA Today Bestseller, Carly Phillips is the queen of Alpha Heroes, at least according to The Harlequin Junkie Reviewer. Carly married her college sweetheart and lives in Purchase, NY along with her crazy dogs who are featured on her Facebook and Instagram pages. The author of over 75 romance novels, she has raised two incredible daughters and is now an empty nester. Carly's book, The Bachelor, was chosen by Kelly Ripa as her first romance club pick. Carly loves social media and interacting with her readers. Want to keep up with Carly? Sign up for her newsletter and receive TWO FREE books at www.carlyphillips.com.

Made in the USA
Coppell, TX
28 August 2024